DISTANT FLICKERS

Stories of Identity & Loss

An Anthology

*With a Foreword
by Amy E. Wallen*

Paul Stream Press, LLC
Nottingham, New Hampshire

ISBN 978-1-7359292-3-1 (paperback)
ISBN 978-1-7359292-4-8 (e-book)

Library of Congress Control Number: 2022911278

Edited by Donna Koros-Stramella & Carol LaHines

© 2022 "A Spoonful of Soup" by Rita Baker

© 2022 "Empty Skies" by John Casey

© 2022 "Norfolk, Virginia, 1975" by Elizabeth Gauffreau

© 2022 "Diary Omissions" by Elizabeth Gauffreau

© 2022 "Hendrix and Wild Ponies" by Donna Koros-Stramella

© 2022 "The Coveting" by Carol LaHines

© 2022 "Two Boys" by Carol LaHines

© 2022 "Where Secrets Go to Hide" by Keith Madsen

© 2022 "The Woman in Question" by Jim Metzner. First appeared in *Running Wild Anthology of Stories,* Volume Four, Book One, 2020.

@ 2022 "Speed Dial" by Amy E. Wallen

© 2022 "Idaho Dreams" by Joyce Yarrow

Visit https://paulstreampress.com Email: contact@paulstreampress.com

CONTENTS

FOREWORD

———◦◦◦———

A DISTANT FLICKER REACHES US like a star, a distant flicker of light. A sharp, quick spark. The stories in this anthology shine each at its own speed of light—dimmer, hidden deep in the darkness, or brighter, burning faster. Through tales of secrets, loss, and identity, empathy illuminates the path, lengthening the shadows of the human emotions laid bare.

When a young boy collects secrets like another boy would collect rocks or stamps, darkness envelops the man he becomes. When a young mother accepts a ride from a stranger, the truth about her situation is revealed to her. A penumbra outlines the dark core of one mother's loss as another mother's gain.

Through stories of divorce, memory lapse, struggles with mental health, and estrangement—loss reveals what we are capable of doing to cope, to recover, to heal, and what we can become as a result—good or evil.

"Out of life's school of war—what doesn't kill me, makes me stronger," Nietzsche wrote. *Distant Flickers* represents the war and the resilience in each human—the light that may be millions of years or a flicker away.

Amy E. Wallen, author of *How to Write a Novel in 20 Pies: Sweet & Savory Secrets for the Writing Life* (AMP, October 2022)

Empty Skies

John Casey

Where
a distant flicker somehow marks
the infinite reach of solitude.
Where a deep, silent nothingness whispers lies
about fading conceptions of hope

and the vast, enveloping black
delivers an invitation to fear.

So easy comes despair.
So easily to tears.

Look closer, nearby, and touch
wherever tears fall.
Where ethereal is real...
Leave others more qualified
to worry for the stars.

HENDRIX AND WILD PONIES

Donna Koros-Stramella

My BLUE JEANS DANCED WITHOUT shame. I held tightly to the waistband of my two-tailed, bell-bottomed kite caught in a wind gust. The dark-green Ford Econoline van navigated onto Route 50, and our speed quickly lifted to 60 mph. My ocean-soaked jeans whipped violently, and I gripped tighter, my thumbs anchored through the belt loops. At that moment, the jeans felt wild and carefree. Unafraid. Just the thought of letting go for once caused me to instinctively pull my jeans partially inside so they wouldn't flutter away.

An hour earlier, my jeans relaxed on the beach—dry and sandy—at least for that moment. I was jumping the Atlantic Ocean's rough, foamy waves with my friends Tony and Suzie as wild ponies watched curiously from the Assateague Island sand dunes.

The three of us were recruited to work for a federal government agency right out of high school. With my parents unwilling to pay for college, the tuition assistance benefit was a gift. The job plunged me into a world of adults, where people talked about drab things like mortgage rates and saving for retirement, inside drab surroundings with grey walls and enormous metal desks. The a.m. radio offered traffic, weather, and news headlines, along with country music—the volume so low it couldn't be heard above the tapping on the (also grey) Smith Corona typewriter.

I was glad to have friends at work who thought more about the weekend than the weekdays. On Saturday, we left before sunrise on our whirlwind day beach trip before Suzie's departure for a three-year assignment at the U.S. Embassy in London.

The sun was still lifting as we crossed the massive Chesapeake Bay Bridge, which united Maryland's eastern and western shores. My hands felt clammy as I looked over the side rails to the deep, quiet bay below. Soon it would be dotted with sailboats, catching the breeze from Annapolis coves and into the open bay. We passed family farms with vegetable and fruit stands edged along the road. We crossed smaller bridges where fishermen shared space with cars. We saw shops offering ice, bait, sandwiches—sometimes all three. Finally, a few road signs came into view—Phillips Seafood Restaurant, Trimper's Rides, Tony's Pizza. We were almost there.

We paid the entrance fee for Assateague Island State Park and parked by a deserted stretch of beach. I had worn my yellow bikini under my jeans and t-shirt, and I stripped down quickly once we reached the shore.

Saturday, July 3. The next day, Americans would celebrate the bicentennial. Today we rocked in the waves, laughing as we surfaced from beneath the churning water after misjudging the sea's timing. Suzie and I were just nineteen, but she looked much younger. She was just five feet, treading water while Tony and I could still touch the sandy bottom.

"Too deep," she shouted above the roar. "Move this way!"

We complied, moving back toward the shore, but the undertow had another idea, and within moments we were out farther than before.

"Again," she said. "I'm tired of treading water!"

"Trying," I said laughing as the sand and the pull conspired against me.

When we finally returned to the beach, the rising tide, or maybe a single stray wave had skimmed over my jeans. By the time we made the twenty-minute drive to Ocean City, my air-dried jeans were stiff, but only slightly damp. We stopped at a roadside stand for a lunch of corn-on-the-cob and Maryland steamed crabs, crowding on the shaded side of the picnic table, letting the Old Bay seasoning deliver a satisfying burn.

We drove further up Coastal Highway, parking near the end of the boardwalk. Tony reminded me of a promise I broke on a cold, late-February day at work. It was his twentieth birthday, and I thoughtlessly forgot my close friend's special day—no card, no gift, no cake. Back then, he had playfully suggested a birthday kiss instead.

"Hmmm, seems only fair," I said, with a laugh. "I did forget your birthday after all."

"What about lunch time?" he asked.

"That doesn't seem appropriate for the office, does it?"

He tilted his head to one side, his brown eyes lighting up as he playfully considered alternatives.

"What about my van?" he asked.

"Meet you there at noon?"

"I'll be there," he said smiling. I shook my head before returning to my desk.

Years later, I learned he wasn't kidding. Tony stood outside his van on the parking lot for nearly an hour, watching coworkers leave and return with bags of sandwiches and fast-food burgers.

Now four months later, he reminded me. . .

"Hey! Remember you promised me that birthday kiss," he said. "Seems like the perfect day."

I played along once again. "OK—let's do it," I said, then turned to Suzie. "I've got to deliver on this birthday kiss. I'll be out in a minute."

"Well, maybe more than a minute," Tony said.

Suzie laughed and sat on the curb as Tony slid open the back door. We sat close to each other on the green shag carpet in the back. I started to say something funny, but he leaned over, his mustache prickly as it brushed my face, his soft lips on mine. This was not a kiss between friends.

He tasted of salt and Old Bay, and we both smelled of coconut from the suntan lotion we'd applied earlier. The ocean was just a block away and I heard the waves pounding outside the van— or at least I thought I did. I'm not sure how much time passed before Suzie knocked on the door.

"Are we going to the boardwalk or not?" she asked.

My face was already flushing. I seldom stepped outside my self-imposed, rigid boundaries. I'd been dating someone on and off for close to a year. I tried breaking it off periodically for a week or so, just to see how I felt. But never a permanent breakup. Gary was a safe choice. He was my date for family events and friends' weddings. He was always available for a last-minute concert or dinner. I was busy with school and friends, and he never seemed to mind being an afterthought. But he increasingly talked about taking our relationship "to the next phase," with hints he'd been looking at rings. I couldn't tell him he wasn't the one. I wasn't even ready to tell myself.

My two friends and I spent the rest of the day on the boardwalk, playing carnival games and eating Thrasher's French Fries doused in vinegar. We sat on the stone wall by the Matterhorn eating our orange and vanilla swirl custard cones, listening to AC/DC and Deep Purple blast from the speakers. This would be the last time the three of us would be together, even though Suzie wouldn't fulfill her three-year obligation. After just one year working for the U.S. government in England, she would resign to play bass in Wicked Women, an all-girl rock band touring Europe.

As the sun set on the bayside, we drove to the outskirts of Ocean City and joined a few dozen people who knew about the secret fireworks' viewing spot. As the first firework lifted, Tony opened all the van doors and pushed an eight-track tape into the player. The three of us sat side-by-side in the damp grass, Jimi Hendrix's ripping version of the national anthem playing at full volume. A couple older men with U.S. Army Vet hats looked over momentarily, then back at the sky.

The night was warm, but not uncomfortable. The sky was clear. My friends were beside me. Summer and the feelings that came with it seemed permanent.

We were quiet on the drive home, just listening to the rest of the Hendrix tape and a few others. Here I was again, still in the sea, the undertow restraining my movement to the shore. I should have been thinking about our past and how everything going forward would be different. And how change could be a good thing. I should have been thinking about my boyfriend Gary and why he was wrong for me. But I wasn't ready. So I thought about the kiss.

Contributor

Donna Koros-Stramella is a novelist whose short pieces have appeared in anthologies, literary magazines, and national online and print publications. She is a previous award-winning journalist and scriptwriter who spent decades as a communication strategist and senior writer in the corporate and government domains. A Maryland resident, she received her MFA from the University of Tampa. Her first novel, *Coffee Killed My Mother,* was published by Adelaide Books in 2020, and she is nearing completion on her second book, *Among the Bones.*

Contributor's Note: "Hendrix and Wild Ponies"

Similar to many of my short pieces, "Hendrix and Wild Ponies," started with a scene drawn from my own life. In this case, a typical sunny beach day that developed into something significant. Unlike other countless days and weeks spent in Ocean City, Maryland that I no longer remember, memories from the day that inspired this story grew increasingly vivid. While capturing that moment in time, I recalled clear, emotive details of the first time I considered a myopic adult life. My fears were not realized. The aperture widened, allowing space for both a youthful spirit and a purposeful life. Over four decades later, I still enjoy hearing Hendrix songs. Not from an eight-track player, but from my husband Tony's guitar.

Book Publication

Novel

Coffee Killed My Mother - Anna Lee is an anxious seventeen-year-old whose life is stuck, largely because of her strained relationship with her mother Jacqueline, a quirky recovering alcoholic who is now addicted to coffee. The two take off on a trip to explore independent coffee shops along the east coast, but Jacqueline's real agenda is an opportunity to reveal a series of disturbing family secrets. The novel's serious study of relationships and the impact of alcoholism are balanced by humor and compassion.

WHERE SECRETS GO TO HIDE

Keith Madsen

———⸺◉⸺———

I STARTED COLLECTING SECRETS WHEN I was just six years old. You ask, "What kind of collection is that for a six-year-old?" I know! I was the only one on my block. Well, at least that was the way it seemed at the time. When you collect secrets, the point is that nobody else knows, so it's impossible to tell; but, believe me, it would not have been my choice of all potential hobbies. My grandma had collected dolls from countries all around the world, and I've always thought that would have been kind of cool for me to do. Yeah, sure, little boys don't do that, but still, to collect a doll from somewhere is almost like experiencing a little what it is like to actually *be* there. I've always wanted to be somewhere else than where I was.

Boys and girls don't always collect what people say they are supposed to collect these days. Like my big sister collected baseball cards. She could outplay most of her guy friends in almost any sport until she reached the eighth grade. That's when her guy friends all seemed to want to collect *her*.

I had other friends and family members who collected stuff, too—coins, stuffed animals, bugs, seashells—you know, normal stuff. And with those collections you can show them off in display cases or on a special shelf in your room. Try doing that with secrets. It's kind of against the whole point of them being secrets.

Anyway, I could have had choices.

Collecting secrets was basically chosen for me. After all, when people start telling you things, or you start observing things you later find out you weren't supposed to observe, and those people tell you to keep it secret, what else can you do with it? You just start collecting them, hiding them wherever they will fit. I used to imagine they all trickled down inside my ear, bypassed my brain, gurgled past my Adam's apple, palpitated through my heart, churning a little in my stomach, before flowing down and nestling into the toes of my Sesame Street pajamas with feet. I figured they would just collect there and stay even when my mom folded those pajamas and put them in my drawer. (But don't think I wouldn't watch her carefully while she was doing that!) If there was a hole in the toe, I would make sure she would sew it up really quickly. Of course, I did wonder how many secrets the toes of my-size pajamas would hold.

You see where this is going, don't you? I thought you would. I don't know whether it was because those pajama feet got all filled up, or because I got older and my feet got bigger, but soon there was no more room in those pajama feet for secrets. Well, that, plus my mother insisted on my getting "big boy pajamas." Yeah, you get it. No feet. My mother hid the old pajamas away as a keepsake, and she would not tell me where.

So, I had to think through other places to store all those secrets which people were making me collect. On observing my older sister, Jessica, I noticed she wrote a lot of things in a little notebook she kept a lock on. One day when I was nine, she left it unlocked, and so I went in her room and opened it up. I mean, I wasn't really being nosy; I just thought that if it helped my sister to write her secrets into a little book like that, maybe I should do it too. So, I opened it up and read something that she obviously wanted to keep as a big secret. I was shocked! She wrote that she had let Bobby Miller get to *second base*! I know! The revelation almost made me drop the book. As recently as when she was in the seventh grade, she had the strongest throwing arm in Valley Middle School. No way any boy was getting to second base on her! At the time I figured she must have let him do it because she liked him or something.

Of course, my sister came back while I was looking at her little book and yelled at me a lot. Then she—you guessed it—she told me I had to keep it a secret. Nobody knows the perils of being a nine-year-old boy without pajama feet.

Obviously if writing secrets in a little book didn't work well for Jessica, it wasn't going to do the job for me, so I had to look for other ways. Someone told me it was always good to entrust your most secret thoughts to God. Of course, I figured God wrote in a book, too, just like my big sister, except his book was called the Holy Bible. I started reading a lot in that book: things about stolen apples, going around naked, throwing a little brother down a well; things I was pretty sure people would have wished God had kept as a secret. And so, at the time I figured if I didn't want the secrets told to me to end up in the Bible, which everyone, even my big sister and my parents read, then I shouldn't tell my secrets to God either.

I've got to say, though, that as I went through my teenage years all of those secrets were getting too much, and I changed my mind and did tell some of them to God. What can you do? My revised theological position was based on a calculation that even though God did write some of those secret things in his book, it wasn't until many years later, so it seemed to me that by the time my secrets made it into the Bible I would already be dead. I haven't encountered the nuances of this theological position in any Bible commentaries, so maybe it's full of holes. Or, I don't know, maybe I'm just that original.

In any case, telling secrets to God really wasn't enough. It helped. But just like taking aspirin after your migraine has already started helps, but doesn't make that headache go away, so it was with my secrets. With no pajama feet to drain into, they just churned around somewhere inside me.

Secrets like my big sister letting Bobby Miller get to second base weren't the tough ones. Even when I got older and figured out what that really meant, I decided letting that secret out wouldn't be fatal for anyone. I mean, for Bobby, all his guy friends would just laugh and chuck him on the shoulder as if he had hit a home run. (And yes,

I am aware of the metaphorical confusion I am getting myself into on that one, but I don't care.) Anyway, the whole thing would not have hurt Bobby Miller. And in the long run, it probably would not have hurt Jessica much, either. Dad would have blown a gasket. Mom would have shed a few tears, but it would have been impossible to tell where those tears had come from—whether from moral regret, memories of her own erratic past, or simply the tears a mother sheds when she realizes her daughter is growing up—or maybe it was all mixed up together in one teary soup, who knows? In the end, Jessica's popularity would have gotten a little booster shot and she would have taken one more turn along the path leading out of the forest of innocence toward the sharp, scraggly peaks of adulthood.

Even from my earliest secret-collecting days it had been impressed upon me that some secrets, were they to be divulged, were far more potent: full of the darkest dread of monsters under one's bed, of thunder rolling with boiling, angry clouds; of cold, steely eyes peering in your bedroom window at night, singeing with frostbite the fringes of your Disney curtains.

People had inflicted me with some secrets like that.

So now I find myself as an adult writing about such secrets and I begin to recoil. If you release a noxious secret into the air, who is there to protect you from its mortal power? Maybe that is why as a child I used to love superheroes. Superman had that x-ray vision that could see past secrets, and no evil villain could stop him from doing so. A person who touched your shame in the darkness could not hide from Zorro or Batman, because the darkness was where they lived. But the cruelest thing they do to you when they make you become an adult is that they take away your superheroes, and make you face the darkness naked and unprotected. And a taunting voice comes out of the shadows, *Who will be your Protector now?*

I guess what is fear-producing about these secrets is that ultimately every secret you collect and hold inside of yourself is ultimately about *you.* I mean, isn't it? If you hold an ugly, dark secret doesn't it say that there is something hidden inside of you that is ugly and dark? What if people saw through the darkness into your naked shame? If secrets hide in your darkness, does that not mean you have chosen to let the darkness be there?

So growing up, for me, ultimately meant talking to someone about all of those secrets. I didn't want to at first. I mean, if I drank enough booze, wouldn't they just pass out of my body with my urine? My sister Jessica convinced me otherwise. She recommended the person she used for her own collection of secrets, a collection I should have known existed, but strangely did not. Once he got me talking, all the secrets became too much and my darkness of heart erupted: *she lied to Grandma and I wasn't to tell he touched me down there Mom wrecked the car I peeked through a crack in the door when Jessica was dressing I cried but he wouldn't stop she was smoking with her friends Uncle Jerry took some whiskey from the cabinet when they weren't around I took the candy from the store and didn't pay Dad kissed the babysitter I paid a girl to do things even though I knew she was going to use the money for drugs I cried and he wouldn't stop Jessica took money from Mom's dresser the boy next door ran outside naked at night I touched her boob on purpose even though I said I didn't I cried and he wouldn't stop Jessica slapped Uncle Jerry's face Mom and Dad had a fight about the babysitter he broke Mom's expensive vase or was that me?*

Now when you collect something normal like baseball cards and they spill all over the floor like that, you can pick them up and straighten them, all with the picture side toward you and with the player right-side up, maybe with players on the same team together, and it's no big deal. But I could tell right away these secrets weren't going back in the deck.

Sorting secrets out in the light of day was much easier than trying to do it in the darkness, though. I guess looking at them without the shadows of fear hiding their edges, without the all-too faint glow of childhood understanding, without the fog created by confused guilt, helps a person sort the innocuous from the spiritually caustic, that which is benign from that which is malignant, that which can be healed by the light alone, from that which requires intense spiritual chemotherapy.

My therapist just kept me talking, and he would smile and nod his head until I realized that all of my secrets had gotten out safely.

Jessica's secrets were apparently more reluctant refugees, but they also made their way out sufficiently for her to agree to marry Bobby Miller. Yeah, at the rehearsal dinner I was asked to give a toast, and so when I raised my glass all I said was, ". . . and he's rounding third and heading home!" I guess Jessica was the only one who got it, because it had been a secret.

I don't miss my collection of secrets, even though I would have to say that when Mom later showed me my old pajamas with feet, in the place where she had stored them, I felt nostalgic. It inspired me to go out and buy some for my own first child, coming next fall.

Of course, I did cut little holes in the toes. My wife doesn't understand, but then again, her family never kept secrets.

Contributor

Keith Madsen is a retired minister who lives in East Wenatchee, Washington with his wife Cathy. He serves with AmeriCorps, teaching English to immigrants and helping low-income families with financial asset-building. He also teaches children and youth chess. He roots for the Seattle Mariners and enjoys the natural beauty of the Pacific Northwest. He has published short stories in *Mobius: The Journal of Social Change, Talking River, Short Story America,* and *Adelaide.*

Contributor's Note: "Where Secrets Go to Hide"

My short story "Where Secrets Go to Hide" evolved from my experience with counseling people as a minister. So many people suffer so much because of childhood traumas they have been told to hide as "family secrets." I believe as a writer that fiction should deal with the tough issues of life, but in a way that brings humor and insight. Otherwise, it just depresses the reader, and nobody is going to read a story that makes them depressed. But when you read about people, people you like and even identify with, who go through tough experiences and come out on top, that lifts you up. It gives you hope. And hope is what I like to write about!

Book Publications

Novels

Searching for Eden - A father mourning the death of his daughter goes to Iran to find the Garden of Eden, where innocence reigned, and death did not exist. Instead, he finds ISIS and Iranian militants. Can he still find his Eden?

The Sons and Daughters of Touissant - Isaac Breda seeks to renew the revolution of his famous forefather, Toussaint Louverture. He is inspired by the words of Margaret Meade: "Never doubt that a small group of thoughtful, committed citizens can change the world; indeed, it's the only thing that ever has." Taking on this challenge transforms both themselves and their country.

NORFOLK, VIRGINIA: 1975 EAST OCEAN VIEW

Elizabeth Gauffreau

THE GIRL WALKED ALONG THE side of Shore Drive carrying her baby on her hip. Her fine blonde hair had grown out of its cut, and every few minutes she pushed the loose ends behind her ears with her free hand. Her face and arms were lightly freckled, and on one side of her neck was a hickey, perfectly round, the size of a dime. Cars rushed by her, and she felt as if their occupants were staring at her. She didn't see any other people walking as she glanced first behind her and then across four lanes of traffic to the other side of the street.

Squids, instantly identifiable by their squared-off military haircuts, thundered slowly past her in brightly-colored muscle cars. Some whistled at her, others made sucking noises, still others hollered, "Hey baby, nice ass! Give me some!" The girl tried to walk without moving her buttocks.

Everything looked dingy and dirty to her—the street, the store signs, the sky, and especially the bars: the Jolly Roger and the Purple Onion which both had tattooed men wearing faded tee-shirts going in and coming out, now, in the middle of the morning. Even her baby looked dingy: the three weeks he'd been out of the sun playing listlessly on the floor with his hard plastic rattles and gummy squeaky toys had turned his midsummer tan faded and muddy.

BethAnn hiked him back onto her pelvic bone and wondered how much farther it was to the Woolco. The sun was hot, and the baby was pushing his hands into her chest.

BethAnn needed to buy a shower curtain because the apartment she lived in had no bathtub, and the shower stall had no curtain. Every time she or her husband took a shower, water sprayed out all over the floor. Afterward she would mop up the water, then get down on hands and knees and dry the floor with one of Donny's old tee-shirts. Last night he had slipped stepping out of the shower, and when he grabbed the towel rack to catch himself, it came off in his hands, screws and all.

"Oh, fuck!" he screamed.

BethAnn, sitting on the sticky vinyl couch feeding the baby a jar of strained apricots, waited for what would come next.

"BethAnn, get in here!"

"I can't! I'm feeding the baby."

"He'll just have to wait, then, won't he? Now get in here!"

"All right. I'm coming." She set the baby on the floor and the jar of apricots in the middle of the coffee table. The baby was smearing them on the couch before she'd gotten halfway across the room.

Donny was lying flat on his back on the bathroom floor holding the towel rack above his head, his head in the doorway, his feet touching the opposite wall. "There's water all over the floor."

"I know. If you'll get up off the floor, I'll wipe it up."

He didn't move or answer, but the towel rack started to shake. BethAnn put her hand in front of her smile. "Why are you lying there like that? You shouldn't have broken the towel rack. We'll get in trouble with the landlord."

"Can't you see that I'm hurt? I fell in this water. Why don't you buy a shower curtain?" He raised himself up on one elbow and twisted around to look at her. "Now, there's a simple solution for you."

BethAnn took the towel rack out of his hand and set it on the back of the toilet. "I can't. We have only five dollars to last until payday."

Donny stood up and, reaching for the towel on the floor, said, "A fucking shower curtain isn't gonna break us."

Later he apologized and showed her the bruise on his tailbone as they undressed for bed, telling her to be careful when they made love.

This morning she'd walked around the corner to Darnell's Variety to buy a shower curtain. The variety store and the moldering Be-Lo Market that adjoined it were owned by the man who owned the Haven Inn Motel across the street and the small cluster of cinder block duplexes she and Donny lived in. When Linda, the girl across the courtyard, had informed BethAnn of this, she had thought that Mr. Darnell must be quite the entrepreneur to own so much property. When BethAnn said as much, Linda snorted and said, "He thinks he is. But we know how he really makes his money." BethAnn opened her mouth to ask how, then closed it, rolled her eyes, and said, "Yeah."

When she asked Mr. Darnell whether he didn't have any shower curtains cheaper than six dollars, he laughed and said, "'Fraid not, sweetheart. What you see is what you get." When she didn't laugh with him, he said, "Try Woolco."

"Where is it?"

"Little Creek Road. You just go down East Ocean View here to Shore Drive, down Shore Drive till you get to the shopping center across from the Amphibious Base. It isn't very far. You can't miss it."

BethAnn paused to adjust the strap of her kidskin shoulder bag, which had slipped off her shoulder and into the crook of her arm. Her parents had given her the bag for her sixteenth birthday two years ago. She'd felt bad about using it at first when it had gotten scuffed and the baby had spit up on it, because it was special, but she didn't think about it anymore.

She hoped Mr. Darnell hadn't sent her on a wild goose chase because she wouldn't buy one of his shower curtains. She'd been walking for almost half an hour and had seen nothing resembling a shopping center, unless she wanted to count a 7-Eleven and a grimy storefront with a bunch of wicker and bamboo stuff in the window. She had never seen so many motels—one every couple of blocks, up and down both sides of the street. She wondered why there were so many, how they could all make a profit located so close to one another like that. This place couldn't get *that* many tourists. When she was five, the family had driven down from Vermont to New Orleans to visit her grandmother, and the first three nights it had taken her father over an hour to find a motel. The first one they'd slept at was one of those tourist cabins.

Her mother stood in the doorway, refusing to go inside. "We can't stay here."

Her father poked his head around her mother's shoulder and looked around the room.

"It's dirty," her mother said.

"No, it's not." Her father set the suitcases down and walked to one of the double beds. He smiled and started to pat it, then stopped as he noticed a couple of dead flies lying in the center of the bed. "Well, maybe you're right," he said, straightening up. "The place is a little on the seedy side. But it'll be fun. We can pretend we're on the lam."

Her mother laughed and brushed the flies off the bed. "On the lam from whom? The school board? Or did they call in the Feds this time? I'd better take Shirley to the bathroom. She's holding herself."

BethAnn trailed behind her mother and sister. At that age she'd loved strange bathrooms, especially those with blue or pink toilets set sleek and low to the floor. As her mother pulled down Shirley's pants and set her on the high toilet seat, BethAnn's attention was caught by a glass on the shelf above the sink, and she reached for it.

"Don't touch that glass!" her mother screamed. "You don't know who's been drinking from it. What kind of germs . . ."

BethAnn had had the same reaction when Mr. Darnell had shown her the apartment three weeks ago. Water pipes ran exposed up the cinder block walls inside, the linoleum floors looked as though they hadn't been mopped since the Second World War, and someone had painted the bedroom furniture with some kind of weird green stuff. The place smelled of cats. She wanted to scream, "I can't live here! You don't know who's been sitting on that couch and eating at that table and walking on that floor. What kind of germs . . . "

But she took the place. It was a hundred and thirty-five a month, all utilities included, they couldn't stay at the Holiday Inn another night, and besides, she was tired. She'd driven the U-Haul van ten hours the day before and had had to sit from ten-thirty until midnight in the pass office at the base waiting for someone to find her husband, while the baby's urine soaked into her lap. The tall, middle-aged man behind the counter kept looking at her and shaking his head. "I've seen this so many

times before, these young kids, so many times."
And she nodded and smiled, trying to be polite,
but wished he would just shut up because he did
not know what he was talking about.

Donny grinned sheepishly as he helped her
into the van. "I got drunk. I didn't think you were
coming. My hair's wet. The guys held my head
under the shower."

"Should you be driving?"

He took the keys from her hand. "Oh yuh, I'm
fine. The walk down the pier sobered me up. You
look terrible."

"Thanks."

"No, really, you look awful."

As he drove to find a motel, she felt relieved
that she was no longer alone in a place where every
street only led to another street and the houses
looked unlike any she'd ever seen before, but she
didn't know what to say to him. He looked different
in his uniform with its white Dixie cup jammed onto
his dripping hair. His long, wrinkled military issue
raincoat looked as if it belonged on someone much
older, as if he were playing dress-up. He smelled
different, too, like machinery and aftershave. She
could think of nothing that had happened to her in
the three months since she had last seen him that
could possibly be of interest to him.

"I missed you," she said.

He put his arm around her and pressed her head onto his shoulder. "I missed you, too."

As she hiked the baby up again and wiped away a bead of sweat trickling down the side of her face, a car pulled up beside her. The driver leaned over to roll down the passenger side window. "You need a ride?" he said. "Where are you going?"

"I'm going to Woolco."

"Woolco? That's a couple of miles from here. Where are you coming from?"

"18th Bay Street."

He opened the car door. "And you're walking to Woolco? Jesus."

She didn't move.

"Come on, get in. I'll run you over there. I'm going that way anyway."

BethAnn thought, *I shouldn't get in the car with him, accepting rides with strangers is dangerous, everyone knows that, and Donny would kill me if he found out, but he won't find out because I won't tell him. The guy looks nice enough, he's probably just being kind. And he certainly wouldn't harm a young woman with a baby in broad daylight.*

Settling the baby on her lap, she glanced over at the man for a closer look. He had strawberry blonde hair feathered back over his ears and a red mustache. His hands on the steering wheel were small and clean.

"That's a cute baby you have there," he said. "A boy?" She nodded.

"How old?"

"Eight months."

Stopping at a light, the man reached over and chucked the baby under the chin. "Cute kid. I have three of my own. But they're all in school now. One's in high school, can you believe that? They don't stay babies for long."

"No, they don't." BethAnn looked at the traffic ahead of them. So many cars.

The man looked over at her and smiled. "Not much of a talker, are you? Think it would help if we were properly introduced? I'm Andy. Who are you?"

She briefly considered giving him a false name—she didn't know why—then told him "Elizabeth."

"Your friends call you Lizzie?"

"No," she said, clutching her pocketbook with one hand and the baby's wet middle with the other.

Andy shrugged and took a pack of Marlboros off the dashboard. He pushed in the cigarette lighter and asked her if she wanted one. She said yes, thank you, and started to reach for the pack, but he took one out, lighted it, and handed it to her.

"So," he said, lighting one for himself. "You're not from around here. Where are you from?"

"Vermont. It's a small town. I'm sure you've never heard of it."

He blew a ragged smoke ring. "I go skiing up in New England a couple times a year. Try me."

"Enosburg Falls."

"You're right. I've never heard of it."

They both laughed.

Leaning his arm across the back of the seat, he said, "I'll bet your husband's in the Navy."

She nodded.

"And this is your first time away from home, right?"

"Oh, no, I used to go to summer camp at Lake Fairlee and once when I was twelve, I rode the bus by myself to visit my grandparents in Maine. It's a beautiful place, Cape Elizabeth. The water is very clean. Cold as hell, though. Turns your whole body blue after ten minutes."

He smiled and turned on his left blinker. "I'll just bet it does. Here's Woolco. See, it is a bit far for you to walk."

She opened the door. "Thank you for the ride. I really appreciate it."

Andy reached into his hip pocket and pulled out a small, white comb. Looking into the rearview mirror, he said, "You get what you need. I'll wait for you here."

"Well, I—"

"I'll give you a ride home. You can't very well walk all that way carrying a shopping bag and a heavy baby. Don't worry. My boss won't mind. I set my own hours."

She took her time buying the shower curtain. She carefully compared prices, quality, colors, and patterns before deciding on a light blue one with white seagulls on it for $2.29. She hesitated on her way to the checkout, looking for the one with the longest line. She headed towards it, then veered off to the one right next it. She really had to get home right away; she'd left the house without making the bed, last night's supper dishes still on the table.

When she walked into the parking lot, blinking in the sudden heat and humidity, Andy was still there. He caught her eye and smiled, and she walked quickly toward his car. After she settled herself and the baby back in, as close to the door as she could get without seeming obvious, Andy lit another cigarette and gave it to her. As he drove, he asked her more questions. How did she like living in the South? She'd just moved here, she wasn't used to it yet. (She didn't tell him that Norfolk was the ugliest place she'd ever seen in her life. Since he did have a southern accent, he might take offense.) Was it hot enough for her? Oh, God, yes. Did her husband go out to sea often? He was due to make his first Mediterranean cruise in five weeks, but she didn't like to think about it.

Riding with Andy in his car, a '74 Monte Carlo with light blue upholstery, BethAnn missed having one. When she and Donny had first started going together in high school, he had been able to use his older brother's car, a '69 Dodge Charger, white and always coated with a thick layer of dust. BethAnn and Donny would go riding around in the Charger every night that she could get out of the house. She would sit close to him on the seat, resting her left hand on his thigh. They would smoke Marlboros and share a Coke from a bottle. Never from a can, it wasn't the same from a can.

They would drive up Main Street and down Main Street, downshifting into jerky first by the park, Donny popping his head out the window and hollering, "Hey, Benoit!" and BethAnn craning her neck to see who Benoit was with this time.

Donny would drive onto a dirt road to park. Some nights he went to West Enosburg, some nights to Montgomery, some nights to East Berkshire. It didn't matter to BethAnn where they went as long as she could look out the car window and see the stars. Her being able to see the stars made their lovemaking much more romantic to her. When Donny was lying heavily on top of her after he had come, his breath panting hot and harsh in her ear, she would rub the condensation from the rear window and stare out at the stars.

Then Donny would drive her home and she would fight with her parents.

When Andy pulled up at her building, she scrambled out of the car and slammed the door. "Thank you very, very much for the ride. I really, really appreciate it."

He got out of the car and stretched both arms above his head. "Aren't you going to invite me in for a drink? It's hot today. And I do have a long drive back to work." BethAnn didn't answer him, and he followed her as she walked to the building. Unlocking her door, she said, "I don't have anything to drink except water. But it's been in the refrigerator, so it's cold."

As she walked through the living room, leaving the front door open, she shivered slightly. Her scalp prickled, and she could feel every individual hair on her head. She knew the cut-offs she was wearing were too short, but she thought she'd be all right—as long as she didn't bend over, not even to set the baby down.

Andy stood in the doorway, looking around the living room. On the orange wall directly in front of him were posters of rock stars: Hendrix, David Bowie with pink hair, the Beatles crossing Abbey Road. He turned to look at the wall behind him. Taking a step closer, he examined two eight-by-ten photographs hanging side by side in matching metal frames. One picture was of a boy in a rented tuxedo and BethAnn wearing a ruffled yellow dress; they were holding hands and smiling. The other showed the same couple, the boy still wearing a rented tuxedo (although not the same one) and BethAnn wearing a big white dress. Each picture had a daisy pressed under the glass. As Andy stepped away from the photographs, he bumped into the coffee table. It was covered with clean, folded baby clothes, magazines, a Monopoly game, and five letters laid out in a row on top of the magazines, all with the same return address in Vermont.

BethAnn stood watching him, clutching the baby tightly to her chest. He nodded at the posters on the wall. "You like rock? I really dig it. Has your old man taken you to Peabody's at the Beach yet?"

She shook her head. "We've just barely gotten unpacked and settled." *Christ,* she thought. *I don't need to make excuses to him.* He smiled at her over the rim of the glass. Finding a bare spot on the coffee table, he set the glass down. "Do you go out?" he said, getting up from the couch.

She cleared her throat. "Some. I take the baby for a walk whenever I can. And I go to the store and stuff."

"No. I mean do you go out?"

Her face flushed and she looked down at the floor. "No. No, I don't."

He stood quietly looking at the top of her head. The baby was fussing and struggling to get down, but she wouldn't loosen her grip on him. He struggled so hard she almost dropped him. Andy picked the glass up off the coffee table, walked into the kitchen, and set it carefully in the sink. Crossing back to BethAnn, he took out his wallet. "Thank you for the water, Elizabeth. It hit the spot." He took a ten-dollar bill out of his wallet. "Here, take this. You need it more than I do."

"But—"

He pushed the money into her hand and turned to go. "Buy something for the baby," he said as he pushed open the screen door. BethAnn bent down and released the baby. When she could no longer hear the sound of Andy's car, she took a deep breath, went into her bedroom, and hid the money in her top bureau drawer.

When Donny got home that evening, she was sitting on the couch, feeding the baby a bottle and watching a Gomer Pyle rerun on TV. As he shut the door behind him, Donny set a small knapsack on the floor. "Those are dirty," he said, pointing to it. She continued to stare at Sergeant Carter holding a troll doll by the hair. "I bought the shower curtain," she said. "It has seagulls on it, and if you don't like it, too bad."

Donny stripped off his sweat-soaked shirt and threw it on her head. "What shower curtain?"

"The baby—"

"I didn't hurt him. Did I, critter?" He tickled his son's stomach, and the baby laughed, milk running out of his mouth and onto BethAnn's bare leg.

Sergeant Carter was ranting about the troll doll. "The shower curtain you told me to buy last night, the shower curtain you ordered me to buy last night, that shower curtain."

Flopping down on the couch next to her, Donny took his shirt off her head and tossed it onto his knapsack. "You did? Really? That's great. What else did you do today?"

"Nothing."

That night BethAnn couldn't sleep. She wanted to take the ten dollars out of her drawer and hide it in a better place, but she was afraid the noise would wake her husband. She got out of bed, slipped into Donny's bathrobe, and tiptoed barefoot into the living room. Crossing to the front window, she pushed the curtain aside and looked out, seeing the same thing she always saw when she looked out that window at three in the morning—the outline of the building across from hers and the largest of the abandoned toys in the courtyard. Then she stood in front of her two photographs and stared at them. She couldn't see them in the dark, but she knew every detail by heart. After half an hour she went back to bed. Donny was lying on his side facing the wall and she pressed herself as close as she could to his back, molding her naked body to his. She put her arm around him and started to cry. Her crying was quiet—just tears trickling from her eyes, nothing more.

Contributor

Elizabeth Gauffreau writes fiction and poetry with a strong connection to family and place. She holds a BA in English/Writing from Old Dominion University and an MA in English/Fiction Writing from the University of New Hampshire. Recent fiction publications include *Woven Tale Press, Dash, Pinyon, Aji, Open: Journal of Arts & Letters,* and *Evening Street Review*. Her debut novel, *Telling Sonny*, was published in 2018. Her debut poetry collection, *Grief Songs: Poems of Love & Remembrance*, was published by Paul Stream Press in September 2021. Learn more about her work at https://lizgauffreau.com.

Contributor's Note:
"Norfolk, Virginia, 1975: East Ocean View"

"Norfolk, Virginia, 1975" is a coming-of-age story based on personal experience. Sadly, it's not a story unique to me. In terms of approach and style, I wrote it during my Raymond Carver gritty realism period. The story can also serve as a time capsule of East Ocean View before urban renewal in the 1980s. While a few of those grim cinderblock houses have survived, the majority of the places in the story are now gone.

Book Publications

Novel

Telling Sonny is a coming-of-age story set in the 1920s, when much of vaudeville had devolved into the Small-Time—but not to a naïve girl from a tiny village in northern Vermont who lets herself be charmed by a cad of a hoofer.

Poetry Collection

Grief Songs: Poems of Love & Remembrance is a collection of photopoetry that tells the story of a loving family lost.

Two Boys

Carol LaHines

———◆———

JULIA BROUGHT THE BABY TO the park every day.
She watched as he chased pigeons and clambered
up the slide; she watched as he filled buckets with
sand, constructing and deconstructing worlds in
the pit. He dug holes in the earth, exposing the
hidden world underneath, the latticework of roots
and deep brown soil. The elms gently swayed,
throwing shadows across the park: the world bleak
and then, suddenly bright, everything a trick of
light and color. When the baby tired, she packed
up their things and left the park, closing the iron
gate behind them.

There was nothing anyone could fault her for; not in any objective sense.

Julia stood on the Forty-Second Street passage, keeping the hair at bay with a hand, feeling the water spit on her face. Tugboats drifted toward the Narrows, and out to the open sea.

She remembered holding Jonah's hand, telling him not to go too close to the edge. Something mothers say, a catechism, *eat your peas, don't jump off the wall, look both ways before crossing the street.*

They left the park and walked to the market. The same errands she always ran, the same bins she rummaged through, looking for a crisp pepper or a ripe cantaloupe. The same checkout girl, the one who used to tell Jonah to give her a high five, low five too slow. "How are you?" the girl asked, not looking at Julia, swiftly packing her groceries.

"Fine," she mumbled. No one wanted to know, not really: the knotty emotions, the sadness at the pit of her. She wondered if the cashier was the one who had cubed the cheeses and julienned the carrots and arranged the platters; the one who'd been on the receiving end of her husband's telephone calls, desperate pleas for meatloaf and mashed potatoes. Julia incapable of mustering enough energy to simply brown some meat or blanch some vegetables.

"We deliver up until ten," the cashier offered. There was always someone on the isle of Manhattan who, for a fee, could pick up your groceries or run your errands, managing the life that had become, for you, ungovernable.

"Thank you, I'll keep that in mind." Julia sniffled.

"Take care of yourself," the cashier said, patting the baby on the head.

"Have a good day," Julia murmured, heading out the automatic doors, into the glare of day.

———

Julia had to contend with many things in recent weeks, not least among them the unruly emotions of strangers and acquaintances. She'd felt responsible, somehow, for their shifts in mood, their dive-bombs into melancholia. Felt it incumbent on herself to cheer them up, to reassure them that everything would be all right. She was coping, going on: what else could she do?

She had to refute the notion, somehow, that the world was a chaotic place. To assure others that what had happened was an aberration. Her very presence—her continued existence—like a negative, the imprint of something left behind.

Meghan had cancelled on her that very morning, citing a middle ear infection or an inner ear imbalance, some condition necessitating a visit to the doctor.

"We'll reschedule," Meghan said, before hastening off the telephone.

Amy, too, had canceled at the last minute, citing a vague familial obligation, an out-of-town cousin or great-aunt who was desperate to go to the Frick. "I'm thinking of you," she said, before hanging up. She'd written the same thing on the note she had included with the tin of shortbread cookies. Fortification that had since grown stale.

"We're going to cross now." Julia maneuvered the stroller around the potholes, and onto the curb.

Felix was a good baby. He was content *to be.* He rarely fussed, and slept for long spells, waking only if hungry.

What a consolation, others had said. *I wouldn't want to think what it'd be like if you didn't have him.* The need to mitigate. To identify the positive aspect, the human interest element of the story. Mother soldiers on through tragedy. Mother finds new purpose in the face of unendurable pain.

He won't have any memory of it, her mother-in-law had offered. No conscious recollection of his brother. Jonah hadn't lived long enough to make a groove in the psyche.

"Let's continue up the hill," Julia said. She spoke often to Felix, though he was barely one. She felt, nonetheless, that she was transmitting something vital, important information about the world: the language of sense, the schematics of emotion. Everything reflected in a mother's expression, in the way she described an oak leaf, or the smooth surface of a rock, *ooh, touch this*, wrapping his tiny fingers around it.

She steered the stroller north, beyond the known boundaries of their world, and east, toward the river, the sea air stinging her eyes. "Sleep now," she hushed Felix, transfixing him with a rattle.

Maybe you might wait until he's older to bring the matter up? Her mother-in-law offered. *What good would it do to tell him? It will just make him feel vulnerable.*

She tucked the blanket into the edges of the stroller. It was spring, but there was still a chill, an air of irresolution; the temperatures fluctuating, difficult to predict from day-to-day. She watched Felix drift off, thumb in his mouth. She watched him sleep, watched as he grunted and shifted and sucked on his thumb. His nostrils gently flaring, the soft rise of his belly.

When she learned she'd be having another boy, others said, *Two boys!*, as if lauding her for reproductive economies. They could wear the same clothes and share the same toys and sleep in the same room. One brother instructing the other in the mechanics of throwing a ball; about tree roots and burrowing worms, the hidden world underneath. They could race each other up the block, chase each other around the trees, exhausting one another before dinnertime so Julia and her husband might have a quiet evening together.

But there were unforeseen events. Julia had learned this when Jonah fell ill. As the gravity of the situation became apparent, as the wave forms on the hospital monitor grew jagged, as she nodded, just to indicate that she was following what the doctors were saying, *Jonah is not expected to recover his system is just too weakened from the septic shock.*

She missed tying his shoes and reminding him to eat his vegetables and the games she played to convince him of the soundness of eating peas and carrots medley. *Umm,* she said, tracing invisible arcs in the air, before landing the fork on his parted lips. She missed saying *don't push,* and *don't wipe your nose on your sleeve,* and *stay out of the puddle,* the one that collected under the park bench when it rained, still water, a breeding ground for mosquitos. She missed tucking him in, lulling him to sleep, whispering *I love you* in his ear, assuring him that the world was not filled with shadowy monsters, or gremlins, *I'll put the light on and you'll see, there is nothing to be afraid of,* just the rustling of the wind and the footsteps of those in the apartment above, *nothing at all to be afraid of, just hush now and go to sleep.* The invisible, glue-on stars on the ceiling, a universe she'd re-created so he could fall asleep imagining himself among the stars.

She sat on a bench along the promenade, watching the barges gliding along the river, passersby hurrying to and fro.

"What a beautiful baby," remarked the woman sitting next to her.

"Thank you." Julia looked at Felix, suckling contentedly. "He's a good boy. Never gives me a problem. Doesn't fuss." He wasn't colicky, or finicky, or gassy; he didn't cry; he didn't wake her in the middle of the night, demanding something she could only guess at.

"How old?" she asked.

"Eleven months," Julia replied. Felix's eyes darted beneath the lids. His fists clenching and unclenching, giving way. The pulsations of an unknown dream. He looked like Jonah, but not quite.

"Is he your first?" the woman asked.

"No," Julia hesitated. "I have one other. Another boy," she said.

"How old is he?"

Julia bit her lip. "Three. He's in pre-school. Just around the block," she pointed. They had enrolled him in a Montessori school in the neighborhood. Julia liked their child-centered philosophy. The emphasis on independence and freedom of movement.

"He must be delightful," the woman remarked.

"He is! He's learning so much now! Letters and numbers and how to trace a perfect circle." Julia looked into the distance. "He loves to construct things. He loves to draw. . ." she trailed off, picturing the runny watercolor Jonah had painted, still on the refrigerator. The spongiform tree. The undulating grass.

"What a wonderful age!" the woman exclaimed. "Every day a new adventure."

Julia nodded. "He's such a chatterbox. He told me that the pterosaur is not really a dinosaur. How do they learn such things?" Julia reflected. The wind skimmed the river, creating small disturbances. She tasted salt on her lips. Jonah had loved the water: the percussive crash of the waves, the sea foam rushing ashore.

"How wonderful," the woman replied. "Two boys!"

"Yes," Julia responded. "Two boys. . ."

She imagined Felix and Jonah together. Running across a field, the light over-exposed. *Mommy, can we play just a little longer?*, rolling across the grass, inhaling the dirt, digging up worms from their underground lairs. *Can't we play a little longer?*, tunneling through the dirt, filling their buckets, promising not to track anything inside. Trapping lady bugs in a jar. And then, miraculously, setting them free, watching them as they flew into the distance, past any known point of reckoning.

Contributor

Carol LaHines is an award-winning author whose fiction has appeared in *Fence, Hayden's Ferry Review, Denver Quarterly, Cimarron Review, The Literary Review, The Laurel Review, Sycamore Review, Permafrost, redivider, Literal Latte* and elsewhere. She is the recipient of the Lamar York Prize for Fiction. Her short stories and novellas have also been finalists for the Mary McCarthy Prize in Short Fiction from Sarabande Books, the David Nathan Meyerson fiction prize, the *New Letters* short story award, and the Disquiet Literary Prize, among others.

Contributor's Note:
"Two Boys"

This is one of the most autobiographical stories I've ever written. I tend not to lift too directly from life (obliquely, sideways—absolutely!) because I am afraid of the narrative distance and necessary scrutiny collapsing. My eldest child died at the age of four, and while I've written frequently of loss, I've really never addressed my own personal loss so directly. The thing about grief is that it estranges you. Your emotions are wild and turbid and entirely your own; others can sympathize and extrapolate but they can never really know what you are experiencing. I didn't want to write an entirely dreary and depressing story. I chose instead to ground the story in the one incident when the narrator speaks to the stranger on the park bench about her children. It is a relief because for once she can be a person without the heft of this past, a person without definition. She chooses to experience a moment of joy, to step outside her grief, to revivify the child in some sense—and so be transported, like one of the ships she watches drifting past on the East River.

Book Publication

Novel

Someday Everything Will All Make Sense, a finalist for the Nilsen Prize for a First Novel and an American Fiction Award, follows Luther van der Loon, an eccentric professor of medieval music at a New York university, as he navigates the stages of grief after his 62-year-old mother chokes on a wonton from a Chinese take-out. The novel speaks to the universality of loss and the struggle to make sense of the nonsensical.

THE COVETING

Carol LaHines

———◦◉◦———

SHE WANTED ALWAYS WHAT WAS not hers. When she was eight years old, she pushed her sister down the stairwell and took her doll—the image of a tortured saint, with a sack for a body and a face carved from a gourd—for her own, claiming divine right. Maria Grazia recovered but was forever feeble, contenting herself with the tiny Magi, the tiny Jesus and donkeys in the crèche, hoping they were too small to arouse her sister's sense of liturgical drama.

But Francesca had already moved on and was plotting to usurp the role of Mary in the village's Christmas pageant from Anna Zoppo, a girl who said novenas as she planted in the fields.

Francesca prayed feverishly for the role, but when her prayers seemed to elicit no response, tricked Anna into placing her hand in the mouth of a boy afflicted with chicken pox. The friars dismissed the pustulant girl, thinking it unseemly for the Mother of God to appear to be afflicted by a pox. And so Francesca assumed the role, parading through the town in blue gown and beaded hood.

Much later, she seduced Alonso Barbarosso, a gold merchant, months before he was to be wed to another. Letting him think that he had impregnated her, and that his soul would be besmirched in Heaven should he fail to legitimize the son she was carrying, she married him at St. Calogero's in a ceremony to which were invited the *prefetto*, the mayor of the village, the *guanti gialli*, the barons and the landholders, and the Franciscan friars, who had remembered the look of impish piety upon the young girl's face. The newlyweds were given a million lire, enough provisions for a holiday on Crete, where—Francesca claimed—the sharp winds, the rough caresses of her husband, and the remoteness of a Catholic church caused her to miscarry.

She did not thereafter conceive. For five years, she maintained that the shock of the miscarriage had upset the machinery of baby-making. Alonso's former fiancée had since wed, bearing her husband three sons, and Alonso, accustomed to indulging his temperamental wife, was becoming suspicious. On the eve of their fifth wedding anniversary, Francesca informed that she was with child. She ran Alonso's hand over a hard sack that she had strapped to her belly, but forbade him to touch her, lest the child be lost to lust and impiety, as was the first.

She bathed sequestered in her room and refused help with getting dressed, lest anyone surmise that she had a lifeless sack strapped to her belly and not a kicking baby; she refused to let the old women of the village rub their hands over her belly and divine its sex, calling their methods blasphemous and an encroachment upon the mysteries of the faith. As she approached her sixth month, the weight of the growing sack upon her, she visited the friary. There she prayed to St. Anthony, who was known to sanction the impossible. When she arrived home, laden with heavy heart and a cask of holy water that she had siphoned off from the friars, she found a letter from her cousin, Carmela Randazza, informing of the impending birth of her seventh child. It seemed as if the mere whiff of Carmela's husband was enough to set off nine months of nausea, relentless *agita*, and a fetus that fought within her for more room and a chokehold upon her bowels. Francesca wrote back, informing her cousin that she would be happy to come to assist with the birth and the care of the baby. She left on the thirty-first of July 1901, with nothing but an old valise and a formless child within her womb.

Her husband tried to forbid the journey, but Francesca was not to be deterred. She traveled for three days, over rocky paths and treacherous twigs, to the interior of the isle where her cousin resided. Never once did she unstrap herself of the growing weight she was carrying, or allow herself to think that it was not that of a child. Traveling thusly, she was reminded of the path of the Christmas pageant, the weight of God, of frankincense and Fool's gold upon her, as she traversed the rocky path from friary to village.

Carmela lived in Naro. She was from a more uncultivated part of the family, content with living in mud houses with thatched roofs and no indoor plumbing, whereas Francesca's mother insisted upon a Neapolitan facade, Renaissance-style ceiling frescoes, and black marble balustrades for her family's home, and traveled to Rome each time she was pregnant, so that her children would be born Romans and not Sicilian peasants. Every time Francesca looked upward as a child, she was reminded, by the lute-playing cherubim and the heavenly host, of her mother's aspirations.

Carmela's ceiling, on the other hand, dripped and sagged under the weight of the mule who liked to sleep on its thick straw.

There was not enough room in the mud house for guests, so Francesca slept next to her cousin. In the darkness, only one oil light illuminating the chamber—nothing more, really, than a bed, a chamber pot, a crucifix and an empty cradle, the same one in which Carmela had rocked her elder sons—Francesca watched the shifting shape of her cousin's belly. The animation of her cousin's uterus only reminded her of the emptiness of her own. Once her cousin chanced to hit Francesca's belly in the restless throes of sleep, remarking that her child seemed like a sack of lard. But she remembered none of it in the morn, and Francesca kept her secret.

Carmela said she had conceived on the feast of the Immaculate Conception. She said it would have been a sacrilege not to let her husband have his way on the day of the Virgin, and so reluctantly delivered herself into his hands. Within a week she felt the wave of nausea and the asphyxiating *agita*, and banished him to the pig stall. He was *en route* to the market in Agrigento, and would not return until after the birth of the baby, when his wife's vengeful hormones had subsided.

According to Francesca's calculations, Carmela's baby was due on the last day of August. But August came and went, and Carmela's baby still fought within her for entrance to the world. The midwife assured Francesca that nature's ways were enigmatic and obstinate and told her to call when the pains started.

Francesca grew certain that God was testing her. She felt more weighed down than the extra flour in her sack could account for, praying nightly to St. Anthony, whom she had chosen as her intermediary to God. *Why is Carmela blessed with six sons, while I am barren?*, she asked, pounding on her belly, in part to break up the clumps of flour that had formed there, in part to assail her useless womb.

Finally—broken by the heat and the unrelenting assault of the fetus upon her bladder—Carmela's waters broke. The midwife had warned that the seventh child would come fast, even faster than the fifth or sixth, who had been delivered on the floor of the mud dwelling and on the way to the outhouse, respectively. Francesca helped her cousin to the bed. There Carmela screamed profanities against the God who had made her and the husband who had razed her spirit with back-to-back pregnancies and philandering in the house of the Lord, the sacristy affording him the privacy he so lacked at home. She cursed the day she was made a woman, and implored God to make of her a wrecked womb, immune to the assaults of men.

"It's too late for the midwife." Carmela clutched her cousin's hand, and begged her to deliver her of her wailing misery.

For a moment, the child stood on the threshold of life, as if deciding whether to enter the world of squalor, impoverishment, and sibling torture that awaited it. He slid out with hardly a push, for his mother's birth canal had so slackened that a sigh sufficed to expel its contents. Francesca clamped the cord and hung the child upside down. Then she swaddled him and placed him in Carmela's arms, where he suckled greedily at the breasts his brothers before him had pummeled beyond shape or allure. Drained of her torment, Carmela fell asleep.

Francesca—stained with blood, mucus, and christened with the infant's first spray of urine— stood at the foot of the bed, watching. The six elder boys had evacuated to a neighbor's at the first labor pain and would not be returning until after the birth of the child. She had mere hours to determine the fate of the infant and the fortunes of the Barbarosso clan, for a son would assure the bloodline, the patrilineal lands, and confirm the righteousness of her and Alonso's marital union.

At last, she pried the infant from his mother. Unbuttoning the dress in which she had concealed her empty breasts, she attempted to nurse him. He rooted wildly, sensing somehow he was mistaken. Francesca rocked him, letting him clamp onto her little finger. And so he quieted, Francesca believed, by virtue of her presence, not knowing that Carmela's milk was enough to sustain him for hours. Finding the vial of holy water that she had carried with her from the friary, that day when she had demanded an answer from God, she drizzled it upon his forehead, saying the Latin blessings that she had learned during her school years in the convent. His soul secured, she rocked him to sleep.

She prolonged her cousin's post-natal stupor by administering laudanum. Carmela slipped into a pleasing semi-consciousness, while the infant suckled and Francesca plotted. She and Carmela were first cousins, making it easier to reconcile the child's appearance. But he had startling blue eyes, a feature not to be found in either her family or the Barbarossos, which she could only ascribe to his philandering father. Still, the eyes could darken with time, or be ascribed to the work of God, who, in so long withholding a son, had blessed them with one of uncommon attributes.

By the time the sun rose, she had made her decision. She summoned the census keeper, to whom she announced the birth of Alessandro Alonso Barbarosso. It was duly recorded in the registry of births, as was the fleeting life of the seventh son of Salvatore and Carmela Randazza. She summoned the priest, who commended her for trying to save the life of her cousin's infant son while in the throes of delivering her own. He was perturbed to find that she had already committed the deceased infant to the ground, but excused the lapse as that of an overzealous Catholic.

Finally, she summoned the doctor, who surmised that seven pregnancies in seven years' time had simply worn out Carmela's womb.

In her haze, Carmela imagined that she had given birth to a howling, robust infant. She felt an ache in her belly and a tingling in her breast, not in the least because Francesca, with no milk of her own, had no choice but to employ Carmela as a wet nurse for her infant son.

Francesca dispatched one of the villagers to Agrigento, to inform Salvatore of the birth and demise of his seventh son. But Salvatore was nowhere to be found, and it soon dawned upon them that he had used his wife's labor as a pretext for desertion. Carmela was secretly relieved to be rid of him, relieved that she would no longer be prey to his fertile lust and philandering miseries, but in her heart, she ached for the infant that was to be the last embodiment of their earthly love.

Lastly, Francesca sent for Alonso. At the sight of the squealing infant he cried for joy, thanking God for his good fortune. He acquiesced in his wife's wish to take with them the grieving Carmela and her fatherless sons, reasoning they could be employed in the upkeep of the estate. And so Carmela continued to nurse her son, unwittingly, until the age of two.

Alessandro Alonso Barbarosso was baptized in Rome. If he was born in the lowlands of Naro, his mother reasoned, he could be baptized in the gothic splendor of a three-nave church, the visages of saints and martyrs gazing favorably upon him. Francesca had felt him growing inside her, as assuredly as if she had nourished him in the sanctum of her womb, had given birth to him as assuredly as if he had squeezed, screaming, through the bony plates of her pelvis, had nursed him as assuredly as if he had suckled at her swollen breasts. He was hers, in the same way that Alonso was hers, or the role of the Virgin Mary, or the doll she had wrested from her sister, long ago.

No other children were born to them. Alonso made his only son the repository of his dreams and visions for the future, and the sole heir of the Barbarosso fortune.

Carmela died before her son reached manhood. Broken by griefs and calamities, she succumbed to consumption. She was nursed, to the end, by her cousin Francesca, who thought it the least she could do for the woman from whom her son, and all her hopes for the future, had sprung.

Before she died, Carmela made a lonely journey to the village of Naro. The mud house had long been abandoned. In it she heard the shrieks and echoes of her chaotic former life, the children running through the rooms and the hurling insults of the marital combatants. She remembered the birth of her last son, his robust cry and rooting for the breast, and could not believe, as she had so long been told, that he had died after two breaths, like a fish out of water. She wandered into the yard, to the marker in the ground, and began digging. She dug until the sun slipped from the horizon, through rocky stones and brambles, through roots and years of sediment.

And still, she found nothing.

Contributor

Carol LaHines is an award-winning author whose fiction has appeared in *Fence, Hayden's Ferry Review, Denver Quarterly, Cimarron Review, The Literary Review, The Laurel Review, Sycamore Review, Permafrost, redivider, Literal Latte* and elsewhere. She is the recipient of the Lamar York Prize for Fiction. Her short stories and novellas have also been finalists for the Mary McCarthy Prize in Short Fiction from Sarabande Books, the David Nathan Meyerson fiction prize, the *New Letters* short story award, and the Disquiet Literary Prize, among others.

Contributor's Note: "The Coveting"

Being adopted, I have always been obsessed with the theme of the lost or appropriated baby. My adoptive parents were Sicilian, and so I am familiar with elements of the culture and folklore. The names of the main characters I borrowed from the names of my adoptive grandmothers (one maintained that she was Roman because her mother would travel all the way from Sicily to Rome to give birth—that element of the story is 100% true). I learned harangues and curse words from that grandmother, who was particularly feisty and often lamented the rigidified customs of her youth. She would "torture" her elder sister Mary, as she described it, pulling pranks and clamping her nose shut with clothespins. As to the Catholic iconography—eleven years of parochial school sticks with you! The immediate impetus for the story was a piece I read in *The New Yorker* by T.C. Boyle. I loved the big voice and the mythic, timeless sense of his tale and aimed for something similar.

Book Publication

Novel

Someday Everything Will All Make Sense, a finalist for the Nilsen Prize for a First Novel and an American Fiction Award, follows Luther van der Loon, an eccentric professor of medieval music at a New York university, as he navigates the stages of grief after his 62-year-old mother chokes on a wonton from a Chinese take-out. The novel speaks to the universality of loss and the struggle to make sense of the nonsensical.

THE WOMAN IN QUESTION

Jim Metzner

———◦◦◦———

IT SMELLS LIKE WHAT IT is, a hospital room cleaned with some serious chemistry.

A window with a bit of a view, a rolling cabinet with a box of tissues, pitcher of water, paper cups and a vase holding some daffodils. A gaze pans to the main attraction, Sophia Marquez, lying on a bed center stage. The woman I married twenty years ago, inspiring poems about bringing candles of love into the cavern of a lonely life.

She's thin and frail. Wavy black hair streaked with grey splaying out across the pillow. Her complexion is smooth; the florescent light of the room sucks the vitality out of her skin, as it does for all life forms, even the daffodils. In her fifties, she's still beautiful, even with her eyes closed.

First time I ever saw Sophia was on China Beach in San Francisco, alone on a blanket twenty yards away, reading a book. Jung, as I recall. At some point she stood up, did a yoga-stretch thing and I noticed her figure—thin arms and legs, narrow waist, generous breasts, long black hair tied in a bun. I thought about going over to her and starting a conversation, but I knew nothing about Jung and her presence wasn't inviting. When I looked up, she was gone. *Another one bites the dust.*

Her eyes open now, blink, and regard me.

"Did you take out the garbage?"

I let out something between a snort and a laugh.

"I think the nurse must have."

"Nurse?"

"You're in a hospital."

"Yes," she says, glancing around the room.

"There was an accident," I say.

"I talked to a doctor."

"Doctor Flenz, yeah. Listen, you want anything? Some water?"

"Yes."

I pour her a cup.

"Thanks. Sammy and Tess?"

"Fine," I say.

Sophia props herself up a little higher on her pillow.

"Where's Sammy?"

"In school. Tess is working at a hairdresser's in town."

"Working? How could she—?"

"You like the flowers?" I ask, scrambling to cover.

"Yes. They're pretty."

"And the garbage, you want me to, uh, take it out?"

"Please."

I pick up the empty wastebasket and walk out of the room, hoping I've dodged a bullet.

Memories. More like burrs than bullets. The events that get attached to your timeline.

Leaving China Beach, I decided on impulse to drive to a movie theater and catch an early show. Settling in with a bag of popcorn in a back row, I noticed the woman I'd just seen lying on a beach blanket walk in and take a seat. The coincidence of running into her again seemed to be a sign from above, if not an outright excuse to enter the fray. I went over and said something exceedingly clever along the lines of, "Didn't I just see you at China Beach?" Her response, a somewhat frosty grunt, left me muttering a few lame pleasantries and heading back to my seat, the dust bitten again.

A few minutes later, she stood up and left; the theater filled and someone took her seat. After the film started, she returned and moved to the front row. I could have just let it lie. Glutton for punishment, I headed down the aisle.

"Saw what happened," I whispered. "There's a free seat in the back if you don't want to sit here craning your neck." She hesitated for a moment and then came to sit next to me.

That was twenty years ago.

Halfway down the hall I see the head nurse. She's busy with her rounds, but she walks over to me, fussing with her clipboard.

"How is your—?" she begins.

"I really need to speak to the doctor."

"You're in luck. He's due on this floor this afternoon. I'll get word to him. Can you stay?"

"If he can find a minute."

"I'll tell him." And she heads down the hallway.

There's a stainless steel fountain; I lean over it hesitating, not wanting to partake in the waters of death. Hospitals have always seemed like that. Put whatever spin on it you like; people die here. That unstated fact hangs in the air; you smell it in the chemicals and breathe it in with the air conditioning.

I try never to be friends with a doctor because it's a lie. You can see it in their eyes. They'd rather be playing golf. One of the first things they're taught in med school is to leave their emotions behind. Otherwise they'd go nuts with all this death. Can't blame them. Doesn't mean I'm going to play along.

An old man wearing a hospital gown pushes an aluminum walker down the hospital corridor moving at a glacial pace, his brown slippers shuffling slowly on the linoleum.

My thoughts ricochet back to that night. After the film it seemed only natural to ask Sophia to go for a cup of coffee.

We strolled from the theater and found a bistro, a little hole in the wall with live Brazilian music. When we walked in, the band was playing a samba. I asked her to dance; she said yes. I was smitten.

I saw her the next day, and the day after that, the Fourth of July. We went on a picnic, ate lobsters, climbed up on a roof to watch fireworks. I asked if I could be her guy. The rest went down like a row of dominos. Moved in together, went camping, travelled to Japan, got married in a redwood grove, landed in upstate New York. Whenever I'd leave for the city, she'd wave good-bye at the window, flash her breasts. I'd pretend to be shocked. Found out we couldn't have kids, so we adopted Sammy and Tess.

Wastebasket in hand, I'm back in the room, trying to remember some of the doctor's suggestions. Get her talking.

"Hottest summer we've had in years," I say.

"They've got the air conditioning on all the time here," Sophia says. "When can I go home?"

"We'll ask the doctor."

"The place is a mess, I'm sure. Are you watering the garden?"

"Anything for the garden," I say. "What do you call that vine with the star flowers, Cla - Clitoris?"

"Clematis. Ooh, you're bad."

"That's true."

"I miss you," she says. "You think there's any way we can—"

"You mean here in the hospital? I, I hardly—"

Sophia giggles. "You look funny when you're flustered. Reminds me of Jerry Lewis."

"The French still think he's a genius."

She touches my hand. "Can we just lock the door or something?"

"You can't lock the doors here. Maybe—"

A nurse enters the room carrying a tray, saving the day.

"How are we doing?" she asks, and I suppress a wiseass response. What is it about nurses that makes you want to give them a hard time, joke around, or entertain some carnal fantasy? For the moment, it's none of the above. She's all business, making sure Sophia takes a pill in the paper cup and downs it with something that resembles orange juice.

"Visiting hours end in half an hour."

"Just waiting for a word with Doctor Flenz," I say.

Before leaving, the nurse checks Sophia's pulse and blood pressure. The whole procedure is vaguely theatrical—the pump, the stethoscope, the starched white costume.

I remember being in Japan with Sophia, watching a Kabuki performance. The faces of the actors were painted, and one woman, a beautiful geisha, wore a mask. At a certain moment in the play, she pulled a string on the bottom of her mask and in an instant was transformed. For me, that image became Sophia. When I told the Kabuki story as a generic anecdote to a friend, she asked, "The woman in question, who could that be?" And the phrase, *The Woman in Question,* stayed with me, like the title of a film Sophia was living in. Now, it feels like I'm cast in the movie without a script, just waiting for that string to get tugged again.

Last week I received a surreal telephone call from Doctor Flenz saying the sleeper had awakened. It was up to me to bring Sophia back from the abyss.

"You look tired," I say. "Want me to wait outside?"

"No. There was something I wanted to ask you, but I can't remember."

"What do you remember?"

"Mostly stuff about you and the kids. Having dinner."

"Which dinner?"

"We're having an argument. Sammy wants to take his plate into the living room to watch television and you want us to all eat together."

"Sounds familiar," I say. "Best guess. How long ago you think that was?"

"I don't know. Last week?" she says.

"You've been in a coma for six months."

"Six months?! Feels like it just happened last week. The dinner, I mean." Sophia takes a few shallow breaths.

"That's hard to believe."

She tries to say something else, but nothing comes. Her eyes go from me to the flowers and the window.

"I'm scared, Will." She reaches out to me, and I hug her, reflexively. I can't help but hug her. When I lean back, her eyes are red and teary.

"I'm going to let you rest now," I say, "until the doctor gets here."

Out in the hallway the guy with the walker is heading in the opposite direction and I wonder if he's doing laps. In twenty years, that could be me. A blue smocked orderly pushes a cot with a woman breathing oxygen through a tube clipped to her nose. She wheels by, her gaze vacant. Maybe she's lost in her own memories. Maybe there's nobody home to think at all. I wend my way to an alcove, read *Travel and Leisure* for an hour and return to the room.

Sophia is propped up on her pillow, a hint of color returning to her cheeks.

"You're looking good," I say, leaning over to kiss her forehead.

"You call that a kiss?" she says, and pulls me close, our lips touching, her tongue exploring my mouth.

I can't quite believe I'm kissing the woman in question. After a minute, I pull away gently.

"Your hair is starting to turn grey," she says.

"Yeah, it started right after the accident."

"Makes you look a lot older."

"Well, a lot can happen in six months."

"I suppose," she says, not sounding convinced.

"I'm hungry," she says.

"I can see that."

"So . . . six months being a long time," Sophia says with a sly smile, "means we have some catching up to do."

"All in good time. You feel like eating something?"

"What have they been feeding me for six months? Baby formula? I'm starving, but I haven't been able to hold down the stuff they've been giving me."

"You have to take it slow. Your body has to relearn how to digest solid food. Nurse told me. Anyway, hospital food sucks. It's another way they encourage you to get out of here."

"I don't need any encouragement," she says, some of the old fire returning to her eyes. "And don't start telling me what to do and what not to do. Six months asleep, two minutes awake and already you're starting, Mister Grey Hair."

"Somebody's feeling feisty. Pretty soon they'll get you up on your feet and you'll be outta here."

"How do I look?" she asks.

"You lost weight."

"I needed to. This wasn't the diet I had in mind."

"You look good," I say. "You really do."

"You're lying. The kids would—" She stops with a worried look. "Who's with the kids now?"

"They're in school."

"But you're here. What about when they get home from school?"

"They can make a snack for themselves. And there's always Mrs. Goldfarb."

"We've got to have the Goldfarbs over for dinner."

I nod my head in agreement, even though the Goldfarbs are gone. Sooner or later Sophia will have to face all that, just as she'll have to face our children.

As if on cue, Sammy and Tess walk into the room with the head nurse behind them, looking concerned. She gives me a helpless glance. It's a shock. They're no longer kids, yet I can't help see them as the culmination of who they have been. Wheeling Tess in her baby carriage at sunset, watching Sammy tackle guys twice his size at a high school football game.

Tess's beautiful auburn hair is dyed black, her eyebrows sculpted. I smile at her and she gives a barely perceptible nod.

Sammy looks like he's been working out. His fists are clenched, as though he's itching to pick a fight. Part of me wants to run over and hug them, while the rest says, *bad idea*. Whatever plan they hatched had gotten them this far, and now it's all improvisation. What do you say to your children when you're feeling pangs of love and remorse for all the ways you could've been a better father, reaping a legacy of mistrust?

"Hello," I manage, trying to sound matter-of-fact but not succeeding.

"What are you doing here?" Tess demands.

"Doctor Flenz asked me to come," I say.

"I think we should have this conversation outside," the head nurse interjects.

"No," Tess says. "We're her children. You can't keep us out."

"Children?" Sophia asks, bewildered.

"It's me, Tess!"

"My daughter has the same name," Sophia says. "She looks like you, but she's much younger."

Sammy takes a step towards me. "What did you do to her?"

I almost laugh, because for years I've wondered what she had done to them.

"We kissed," I said.

Again, the nurse starts to speak, but Sophia interrupts her.

"Will, what's going on here?"

If only fate would intervene and bring Dr. Flenz to save us all. In negotiations, they say whoever speaks first loses. All eyes are on me.

I flash back to standing in a courtroom, listening to a judge bring resolution to a year of legal warfare, grateful the ordeal was finally ending.

I wonder if Sophia will ever remember that. I know I can't forget.

"You lost your memory in the accident," I say, "a big chunk of it, more than you realize."

Sophia is staring at me intently, incredulous.

"When you came out of the coma, you asked for me. That's why I'm here. Doctor's orders. I'm the one you're supposed to talk to first. Everything I'm saying you would have learned sooner or later. So now it's sooner. This is Sammy and Tess."

Sophia's hand flies up to her mouth. I'm thinking maybe I should stop, let it sink in, but the words pour out unbidden.

"You and I got divorced ten years ago. It was bad, brutal."

I'm crying again, just as I did in the courtroom. I walk over and commandeer a tissue from the bedside.

"Divorced?" Sophia says, tasting the word. I nod.

"The children love you. They've stuck by you. It's been harder for me. We became enemies. For what it's worth, I've forgiven you."

In the silence of the room, the clock, which had been ticking all along, becomes audible. Ten seconds of ticks can seem like a long time.

"Nice," Tess says. "You were always good at giving speeches."

"Hold it," Sophia says, "hold it right there."

Whatever Tess is feeling, she's keeping a lid on it. Sammy is pacing slowly, like a leopard.

Sophia closes her eyes and speaks softly, as if she's talking on the phone.

"A bad dream."

She opens her eyes, takes a sip of water from the cup at her bedside and looks at me.

"So all of this, the last two days, the kiss—which I *do* remember—"

"—was to bring you back," I say.

"Back to what? Divorced? This is the truth, what you're saying now?"

"The truth," I say, glancing towards the kids.

"Yeah, it happened," Tess says.

"Was it really that bad?" Sophia asks.

"Horrible." And it was. A legal bloodletting with the smallest issues taken to the mat. At the end of the ordeal the only ones smiling were the attorneys.

The color is gone from Sophia's face, replaced by a look of total despondency. I can't imagine what this must be like for her, everything turned upside down in an instant. If only the kids hadn't shown up when they did. Maybe it's better that it happens now. The woman in question is moving her lips, either praying or convincing herself of something. Then she seems to rally a bit and unless I'm imagining it, there's a glint in her eye.

"I suppose I'll have to speak to a lawyer or look at the papers, whatever you call them," Sophia says, her hands tightening on the bed sheet.

I hold my breath, not wanting to know what might come next, the wound inside itching to bleed again.

Sophia takes stock of Sammy and Tess.

"Ten years, huh? Unbelievable." Tears well up in her eyes. "You've grown up. Of course you have. What a stupid thing to say. I haven't grown up, have I? Tell me something." Her eyes go wide and wild. "Who am I? Can any of you tell me that! Who am I, for Christ's sake?"

No one answers. I'm numb. Sammy's scanning the room for someone to blame. Tess reaches into her pocketbook for a Chapstick. The head nurse, resigned to be a designated witness, stands with her arms folded across her clipboard.

Sophia looks abashed. "Sorry," she says. "Don't be scared, I'm still your mother. That much we know." She shivers and pulls the bed sheet up a little higher. "I don't know whether to laugh or cry. Maybe the doctor can tell me. But you two. So big. You'll have to catch me up. Come here, I won't bite."

They approach warily and Sophia hugs each of them, kissing Tess between her eyes and rubbing Sammy's crew cut with her knuckles.

"Payment in advance, no—arrears," she says, her hands on Sammy's shoulders. "Look, if you really love me like your father says—"

"He's not my father," Sammy interrupts.

"If you really love me," Sophia continues, "then you're going to have to give me some time. Last time I knew you was a long time ago." She's hugging herself now, rubbing her hands up and down her arms like she's trying to warm up.

"Must sound strange to hear your mother say that, but it's true, unlike what I've been hearing the last couple of days. I don't know who the two of you are. And God knows, I don't know who *you* are, Will. Divorced! Well, if you can lie as good as you've been doing, then I guess I can believe anything. Maybe I'll wake up and it'll be different." She shakes her head. "Ten minutes ago, we were lovers! You think I can just turn that off?!" She snaps her fingers. "What about you? Is it really all over?"

I'm thinking she's the lucky one. No divorce, no battleground, only the good stuff. What would it take to wipe my hard drive like that, forget who Sophia became and fall in love again with the woman I met at the beach? The kids are looking at me expectantly, like this could be some Disney flick where everything turns out right in the end. I'm trying to find a word, one word, that would be true and right. I feel like the guy in the walker. Everything has slowed down. Anything could happen now. Anything.

I take a deep breath and that smell, the hospital smell, is gone. Maybe I've just gotten used to it.

I walk over to the bedside and reach for Sophia's hand. She squeezes it very lightly. I'm wondering if it's not the things we say that really matter, but everything else that's hanging in the air, the possibilities that live amongst us, the questions unanswered.

"I don't know what to think anymore," Sophia says. "When I wake up and this is still real, I'll let you know." She closes her eyes and seems to drift into sleep.

Contributor

Jim Metzner is a sound recordist and radio producer, best known as the host of the Pulse of the Planet radio series and podcast. He's currently working on a memoir, "Adventures of a Lifelong Listener," which weaves together sounds and stories to explore the mystery of listening.

Contributor's Note: "The Woman in Question"

What's the impetus behind this story? "The Woman in Question" presents a scenario I wanted to explore: what if a person who had gone through a brutal divorce suffered memory loss? How would that play out for both parties?

Book Publication

Novel

Sacred Mounds is an adventure tale which explores the mystery of the ancient earthworks that once proliferated across the eastern US. The novel is a finalist in the Screencraft Cinematic Book Writing Competition. Its foreword was written by Hutke Fields, principal chief of the Natchez Nation.

DIARY OMISSIONS: THE HOUSE ON EDGEWOOD ROAD

Elizabeth Gauffreau

———◦◦———

April 17, 1907–June 1, 1907

BROTHER AND I WERE STILL so very young the first time Father took Mother away, not long after we moved into the new house on Edgewood Road. Father had designed the house himself, and it was *big*—not as big as Uncle Henry and Aunt Lucy's grand house on the hill, of course, but it was big for us, with four bedrooms, front and back porches, and a sunroom looking out through the trees.

Father was so proud of that house. While it was being built, he would take us to see it every Sunday after church, all of us dressed in our Sunday best to gaze at the hole in the ground, then at the outlines of walls and roof empty against the sky.

The day began the same as any other. We saw Father off to work in the morning as usual, the three of us each receiving a kiss in turn at the door before he set off smartly down the walk, his portfolio tucked under his arm, his hat tilted just so.

Brother and I ran upstairs while Mother cleared the table and began the breakfast dishes. I heard the hot water running downstairs, the heavy plates thunking on the bottom of the sink, the silverware rattling in on top of them.

Ready for play, Brother and I ran down the front stairs and through the hall, slowing the clattering of our shoes as we reached the shiny kitchen linoleum. Mother stood motionless at the sink, the plates and bowls arranged in descending order in the dish drainer on her right, a stack of greasy pans on the counter on her left, the suds gone from the water, her red wet hands resting on the rim of the sink, tears running down her face.

I stopped and asked what was the matter, was she sick, was she sad, but she shook her head and motioned with her hand for me to go away.

When Brother and I came in for lunch, we found that Mother had not moved from the sink, the water gone cold in front of her, the tears dried on her face. She did not answer when I called her. Brother ran up the hill to Aunt Lucy's house because he was younger and more afraid, while I stayed behind with Mother, crying, unable to pull one of her hands down from the rim of the sink to hold. Aunt Lucy telephoned Father in the city, and he came home and took Mother away.

Cousin Charlotte came to stay with us. We didn't like Cousin Charlotte much. She was prissy, and the only reason she'd come to help us while Mother was away was that Aunt Lucy made her. When Brother and I asked where our mother went, why Father took her away, Cousin Charlotte said that Mother needed a rest. When Brother demanded to know why Mother couldn't take her nap at home, Cousin Charlotte called him a naughty boy and sent him to his room. Then she sent me to my room, too, just for good measure.

When at last the day came for Father to bring Mother home from her rest, Brother and I ran to the door at the sound of the auto in the drive, but Cousin Charlotte grabbed our hands and pulled us back. She held tight to our hands as the door opened and Father led Mother inside and up the stairs.

Later, when Cousin Charlotte went into the kitchen to make supper, Brother and I tiptoed upstairs to see Mother. We found Father sitting against the head of the bed reading aloud from a book while Mother lay on her back with her eyes closed. Father didn't notice Brother and me standing in the doorway, and we went back downstairs.

Father took his supper with Mother in their room that evening, while Brother and I ate downstairs in the dining room with Cousin Charlotte. After a few days, Mother was back to taking care of us, and Cousin Charlotte went home to Aunt Lucy and Uncle Henry's big house on the hill. We went back to seeing Father off to work in the morning as usual, the three of us each receiving a kiss in turn at the door before he set off whistling down the walk, turning to wave before he disappeared from sight.

May 17, 1917–July 2, 1917

The second time Father took Mother away, Jimmy and I were older, in junior high school. We had been living in the house on Edgewood Road for ten years, and the month prior, Father had taken it into his head that the floors needed to be refinished. We spent two weeks with Uncle Henry, Aunt Lucy, and Cousin Charlotte in the big house on the hill. When the work was finally completed, Jimmy and I couldn't run down that hill for home fast enough.

Father still left the house early each morning to catch the train into the city, setting off smartly down the walk, his portfolio tucked under his arm, his hat tilted just so, Mother still receiving his kiss at the door, Jimmy and I too busy shouting at each other for our turn in the bathroom and shouting at Mother to find our missing homework to be bothered.

So off to school we dashed that day, Jimmy and I, bag lunches snatched from Mother's hands, our breakfasts untouched on the table. Returning home late in the afternoon, after dawdling over strictly-forbidden ice cream sodas at the drugstore, we found a pile of something white on the curb in front of our house. When we set our schoolbooks down to investigate, the pile turned out to be sopping wet bed sheets.

We could see where a trail of water had dried on the front walk. Water still puddled on the front porch, and the trail of water continued down the front hall, through the kitchen, out the kitchen door, and onto the back porch, ending at Mother's brand-new, gasoline-powered Maytag washing machine. The lid was open, and the tub was half full of water.

I grabbed a string mop out of the pantry and mopped up the puddles of water as quickly as I could while Jimmy searched the house for Mother. Before long, he shouted from the top of the stairs, "Her bedroom door's locked!" By the time I put the mop back in the pantry, he had gone from gently knocking on the door and calling, "Mother, Mother? Are you in there? Are you all right?" to pounding on it and yelling, "Open the door, Mother!"

I ran up the stairs. "Do you know she's in there?"

"Of course, she's in there, stupid—the door's locked from the inside!"

"Is she all right?"

"I don't know!" He knelt down and peered into the keyhole. "The key's still in the lock."

I ran to my closet and retrieved a coat hanger. "Here, help me bend this." We somehow managed to straighten the hanger enough to dislodge the key from the lock and sweep it under the door. When we unlocked the door and entered the room, I nearly fell over Mother's clothes on the floor. She was lying naked on the bed staring out the window. I shouted at Jimmy not to look and threw a blanket over her. Then Jimmy and I both stood in her line of sight, blocking the window as we begged her to tell us what was wrong, was she sick, had she hurt herself? Why was the washing on the curb? Why were her clothes on the floor?

Then we heard footsteps pounding up the stairs, and Father sent us from the room while he asked Mother the same questions we had. What was wrong, was she sick, had she hurt herself? He didn't seem to care about the washing on the curb or her clothes on the floor.

Jimmy and I stood at the bottom of the stairs listening to Father plead with her in vain. Finally, he walked back down the stairs and called the doctor. After the doctor came, he and Father got Mother dressed, down the stairs, and into the doctor's car, without a word to Jimmy and me. As they drove away, I looked at Jimmy and said, "I guess we'd better get the sheets off the curb." Between the two of us, we got the washing machine started, the sheets washed, rinsed, pushed through the wringer, and hung on the clothesline.

By the time we finished, it had gotten dark, and we'd missed supper. I found leftover ham in the icebox and made us ham sandwiches. I made one for Father, too, which I covered in waxed paper and left in the icebox. Then Jimmy and I did our homework and waited for Father to return. He told us Mother just needed a rest. For how long? He didn't know.

When Jimmy and I got home from school the following day, Cousin Charlotte's suitcase was in the guestroom, and Cousin Charlotte was in the kitchen folding towels. "Too bad about your mother," she said. "The hall floor is going to have to be refinished. The varnish is ruined."

What were Jimmy and I supposed to say to that?

When Father brought Mother home more than a month later, Jimmy and I asked if she might like to change washing day to Saturday, so that we could help her with it. She shook her head and started to cry, which wasn't what we had intended at all. Father told us not to upset her and took her upstairs.

While the hall floor was being refinished, we stayed at the Puritan Hotel and took our meals in the dining room. I don't know what Mother did with her time while Jimmy and I were at school and Father was at work, but she seemed cheerful enough, and when we returned home, things went back to normal.

May 1, 1920–

Jimmy and I were nearly grown the next time Mother needed a long rest. The house on Edgewood Road had just received all new wallpaper, Father having decided that the original wallpaper was faded and shabby. At least we'd been able to remain in the house while the work was being done.

All semblance of a morning routine was long gone by then, Jimmy and I barely rolling out of bed in time to make it to the high school for first period bell. The one remaining constant was Father's kiss goodbye for Mother before he set off down the front walk with his portfolio under his arm, his hat tilted just so.

I was late getting home that day, having stayed after school for a yearbook meeting. Jimmy arrived shortly after I did, from baseball practice. It was nearly suppertime, but there was no smell of roast or casserole coming from the kitchen, although a pot of potatoes in water had been set on the back burner of the stove. Mother was nowhere to be found in the house or the backyard. Jimmy even checked the potting shed, but it was padlocked from the outside as usual.

"Maybe she ran out of something for supper and nipped down to the store?" I said when Jimmy returned from the backyard.

"Maybe . . . " He looked doubtful. "What should we do? Should we check with the neighbors?"

"We'd probably best wait for Father," I said.

So that's what we did. We sat at the dining room table trying to concentrate on our homework, which would come due in the morning, missing mother or no missing mother.

When Father arrived home, he called out, "I'm home, Leona!" as he set his hat on the hall tree and leaned his portfolio against the wall. We heard him proceed to the kitchen to greet Mother and perhaps steal a sample of what was for supper. We heard him open and close the door of the icebox, open and close the door of the oven. We heard him go upstairs to their bedroom, come back downstairs.

"Where's your mother?" he said, entering the dining room.

"We don't know," I said. "She wasn't here when I got home."

"Or when I got home," Jimmy said.

"Have you called Aunt Lucy?"

Jimmy and I shook our heads, both of us knowing for a certainty that Mother was not about to go anywhere near Aunt Lucy and Uncle Henry's big house on the hill.

Father telephoned Aunt Lucy and confirmed what Jimmy and I already knew.

"Have you tried the neighbors?" Father said, his expression saying he hoped we hadn't.

"No, we thought we should wait for you."

"I can't think where she could have got to," Father said. "We'll have to try the neighbors."

The three of us canvassed both sides of the street with no luck. The last time any of the neighbors had seen Mother was the previous day when she was out in back doing the washing.

Father called Aunt Lucy, Uncle Henry, and Cousin Charlotte to the house for a family meeting. Should he call the police? Should he not call the police? Worry won out over propriety, and Father called the police. Aunt Lucy and Uncle Henry immediately stood up to leave, while Cousin Charlotte stayed right where she was, in Mother's favorite armchair.

"Come, Charlotte," Aunt Lucy said. "This is a private matter between your Uncle Willard and the authorities. They certainly don't need an audience."

When the police officer arrived, he asked about Mother's habits and state of mind. Was she a woman of regular habits? Had anything been troubling her? Had she ever done anything like this before? To my surprise, Father answered honestly. Leona was mostly a woman of regular habits. At times she was troubled, although she had never left the house with no word to anyone. The officer wrote Father's responses in a little notebook. Then he asked Father what Mother looked like.

"She's a beautiful woman," Father said. He looked surprised when the officer didn't write it down.

I stood up. "My mother and I are the same height and build. Her hair is darker than mine, with grey streaks in the front."

"Thank you, miss." The officer wrote in his little notebook again. He put the notebook back in his pocket and asked for a recent photograph. Father got up from his chair, took Mother's latest studio portrait from the mantelpiece, and thrust it, still in its ornate silver frame, at the officer.

"Oh, I don't need the frame, sir."

I quickly interjected, "We have a smaller one," and ran upstairs to get it from Father's nightstand, slipping it from its frame before leaving the room. After I'd handed the photograph to the officer and he'd slid it carefully into his jacket pocket, Father tentatively cleared his throat and said, "What should we do now?"

"I'm afraid," the officer said, settling his hat back on his head and turning to leave, "there is nothing for you to do but wait. I'll check the hospitals for you when I get back to the station."

"Hospitals?" Father said.

"Just in case she's been hurt or suddenly taken ill."

"But if she'd been hurt or taken ill, someone would have called me. Or my sister Lucy. Everyone knows us."

"Yes, sir," the officer said. "Give me about an hour to make the calls."

Father closed the front door behind the officer and sat at the tiny telephone table in the hall. Jimmy and I looked at each other, unsure what to do. I looked at my wristwatch. "It's after eight, Father," I said, "and we haven't eaten. Let me make us some sandwiches."

"Thank you, dear. I'll take mine here."

Jimmy and I looked at each other again. He followed me into the kitchen and sliced the bread for me, his hands steadier than mine, as we whispered back and forth about what we should do about finding Mother, what we should do about Father sitting so forlornly in the front hall waiting for the telephone to ring. After I made the sandwiches, we brought our plates into the front hall, handed Father his, and sat on the floor to eat our sandwiches and wait with him.

The telephone never rang. Instead, at close to midnight, a knock came at the front door. Father got to the door first, and when he opened it, there was the police officer from earlier in the evening, with his arm around Mother. Her hair was disheveled, she was shivering, and she wouldn't look at any of us. Father let me take her upstairs while he spoke with the police officer to find out where she'd been. Mother didn't speak to me, but she knew who I was, and she let me run her a hot bath and help her out of her clothes. Father came upstairs, and I went back downstairs to find out from Jimmy what had happened.

The night janitor at the Central Library had found Mother asleep in the stacks, her back against the wall, an open book on her lap. The janitor didn't know what to do, so he called the police to come and get her. She didn't offer any kind of explanation to the police. Apparently, she had peeled potatoes for supper, put them in a pot of water on the stove, then walked out the door and took two streetcars to the Central Library to hide herself in the stacks and read.

Father didn't take Mother away this time. Every night, when he got home from work in the city, he went straight upstairs to sit with her, preferring to have her with him, her empty gaze turned inward, than not have her with him at all. Somehow, the three of us would manage the house on Edgewood Road until Mother was ready to resume her place in it once more.

Contributor

Elizabeth Gauffreau writes fiction and poetry with a strong connection to family and place. She holds a BA in English/Writing from Old Dominion University and an MA in English/Fiction Writing from the University of New Hampshire. Recent fiction publications include *Woven Tale Press, Dash, Pinyon, Aji, Open: Journal of Arts & Letters,* and *Evening Street Review.* Her debut novel, *Telling Sonny,* was published in 2018. Her debut poetry collection, *Grief Songs: Poems of Love & Remembrance,* was published by Paul Stream Press in September 2021. Learn more about her work at https://lizgauffreau.com.

Contributor's Note:
"Diary Omissions:
The House on Edgewood Road"

"Diary Omissions" began life many years ago as part of a failed novel. The initial inspiration was family photographs and a 1906 diary left by a first cousin twice-removed. I revised the story several times to develop the setting, characters, and plot more fully. "Diary Omissions" is one of several stories I've written about women who are unhappy in their expected social roles.

Book Publications

Novel

Telling Sonny is a coming-of-age story set in the 1920s, when much of vaudeville had devolved into the Small-Time—but not to a naïve girl from a tiny Vermont village who lets herself be charmed by a cad of a hoofer.

Poetry Collection

Grief Songs: Poems of Love & Remembrance is a collection of photopoetry that tells the story of a loving family lost.

Idaho Dreams

Joyce Yarrow

———◦❈◦———

CORA WOULD NEVER HAVE ADMITTED this to Damien, but there were times when she missed Seattle so much that traces of salt air flowed through her nostrils and she heard a faint ferry horn in the distance. On such mornings the interminable blue sky of Idaho threatened to drive her mad and she was haunted by the blurred faces of old friends. Oh, to be able to return to bygone haunts like the Zeitgeist Cafe, where she took breaks from teaching aerobics at the fitness center near King Station.

The smell of burnt eggs and the sight of Henry and Hannah whooping it up on the tree swing out front brought her back to the present and the farmhouse that for two years, like it or not, she'd called home.

Switching off the gas burner, Cora scrubbed the charred remains off the frying pan and started over. When the toast popped up, she opened the screen door and yelled, "Come and get it before the crows do!" This was not as unlikely as it sounded. When they first arrived on the farm their house had still been under construction, with only a light tarp for a roof, inviting birds and insects to invade in search of food. Even then, she envied their freedom to come and go as they pleased.

Henry sprinted over the lawn and made it to the porch ahead of Hannah, holding the door open for his sister. He'd inherited Damien's thing for manners as well as a strong need to take full control of every situation. Like when D—who had been out of town for a week wiring an industrial park—walked into their vintage Seattle loft and stated flatly, "We're moving to Idaho. I found us a farm."

"Just like that?" For Cora their rural dream had been a shared fantasy, like traveling to Europe or buying an expensive electric car.

"Isn't it what you've always wanted? To leave the city and grow our own food?"

It was true. They'd met three years ago on a Farm Walk sponsored by the Tilth Alliance. Aside from gardening, the favorite activities of the man she'd fallen in love with had been square-dancing and kayaking. And doting on his two precocious children, who he told her had lost their mother to a drug overdose. He treated the kids like miniature grownups, instructing them on the Latin names for the radishes (*Raphanus sativus*) and peas (*Pisum sativum*) that he helped them plant in their section of the tiny urban garden that grew behind their equally tiny house.

Until the day he gave his ultimatum, she'd thought Damien enjoyed living in the Emerald City as much as she did, that they were a committed couple who made important decisions together, from choosing a new washing machine to picking out new bedroom curtains. But this time Damien made it clear he'd made a firm decision and was moving with or without her. He would take a few weeks to get the place ready, he said—there was some construction he needed to do—and then he'd come back for the children, who by then belonged every bit as much to her as they did to him. Because she loved him and maybe the kids even more, Cora saw no choice but to surrender.

And now that their dreamworld was feeling more like a prison than a refuge, she wished she'd taken a stand.

She tossed the heavy thought overboard and aimed a practiced smile at Hannah, an elfin prankster with a mane of jet-black hair, who liked to pile her eggs onto a slice of toast and stuff the whole, soggy burrito into her mouth. Henry was at the other end of the spectrum, an obedient son with a habit of balancing a textbook in one hand while carefully feeding himself a forkful per paragraph with the other. They balanced each other perfectly.

Cora told herself that the gift of Henry and Hannah's presence in her life was far greater than any sacrifices she'd made for them. She might feel tempted at times to abandon Damien, with his mood swings and inexplicable demands, but she would not break the children's hearts again. They'd already lost one mother.

It was Henry's turn to wash up. He frowned and squinted against the glare in the kitchen window, running the soap-filled brush over his sister's plate as the sun streamed in, sending an invitation they knew they couldn't accept. Damien was adamant about the family staying indoors when he wasn't around. If he discovered that Cora had let the children out to play before breakfast. . .

"Who's that in the orchard?" The boy's voice was not as nonchalant as he wanted it to sound.

For Cora, one look was enough. "Under the table! Now!" she ordered.

She activated the wall switch, closing the metal blinds and plunging the kitchen into darkness. Then she felt her way along the wall and reached inside the closet next to the cellar stairs for the satellite phone.

"Cora. What's happening?" Henry's already high voice had gone up an octave.

"Don't worry. You know your father has strict rules we follow for trespassers but that doesn't mean we're in any danger."

This was the first time she'd carried out Damien's instructions. When he installed the special shades he'd made light of it, saying, "When your nearest neighbor is miles away you'd better have a good plan B."

Some alarm bells had gone off for Cora. Wasn't this a little extreme? On the other hand, she was touched by her husband's concern for the safety of his family. Had his paranoia become contagious? After all, she was often at home alone, homeschooling the kids, while his work as an electrician took him far and wide. So far, any plans to steal a few hours to teach a fitness class in the community room of the church in Packer's Ridge had come to naught.

Ten minutes after Cora's call, Damien—who was working close to home that day—drove his truck right up to the foundation of the house and jumped out.

"What the hell are you doing on the porch?" he shouted. "Cora, we went over this."

"I wanted you to know first thing that we're all okay." She spoke in the same patient tone she'd used when instructing women at the gym: "knees up, shoulders, straight." Why the presence of one stranger on their land was cause for immediate panic was a mystery she'd given up on trying to solve. What else do you do when someone you love becomes someone you're afraid of who answers all your questions with, "Don't ask unless you really want to know."

She went inside to reassure the kids while Damien hiked the perimeter. "Twice, just to make sure the guy is gone," he told her when he returned, swapping his muddy boots for the deerskin slippers he kept on the porch.

He was a whiz with technology and electronic sensors—no barbed wire or high fences—just a small *Keep Out* sign at the turnoff to the driveway. The electric eyes were well below eye level and hard to detect unless you knew what you were looking for, yet somehow, they had failed to pick up the intruder.

"There's a flaw in the system. I should have gotten a message on my phone," Damien said.

"Our intruder must have used an infrared reader so he could step over the beams undetected. Not a good sign."

He tried to hide his panic and disappointment but Cora knew that look. She'd seen it on his face when he announced their mandated move to Idaho. If they left the farm, she would miss the life they were creating for themselves. They'd planted a sustainable vegetable garden as well as a line of tall birches to keep the scrub oaks company. Their Jonagold apples continued to sell and she'd made one or two friends in town despite Damien's ban on invitations to coffee.

She wasn't sure how, but this time she'd find a way to prevent him from hitting the reset button. She might not like it here much, but Damien was finally talking about allowing the kids to register for school. Hannah would be in first grade and Henry in fourth. If only Damien would calm down a little and let them lead a normal life. The soil was good here. Maybe they could put down some roots.

When they'd moved here, the residents assumed this new family was just another self-contained, antisocial unit seeking isolation and cheap rent. Damien did nothing to discourage that perception. "Welcome, we won't bother you much," was the first thing out of the clerk's mouth when D rented a postal box. Followed by "can't be too careful," when Damien told her the PO box would be in his wife's name.

Cora resented this misrepresentation of who they were. Why the subterfuge? Why was her husband painstakingly assuming all the trappings of a survivalist? She watched in dismay as he bought a huge stock of ammo at the local hardware store and stocked up on canned goods. And then, as if to add a finishing touch to her unease, she'd discovered—while cutting back some noxious branches of poison oak on a hillside—a steel door set into a slab of concrete on the hillside.

She had called Damien on his cell. "You'd better come out and explain this. It looks like the entrance to an underground bunker."

Striding across the field toward her, he'd slowed his pace and grinned when he saw her watching. Suddenly she'd doubted every single thing she knew about him.

"It's designed to keep the neighbors happy," Damien explained when he got within hearing range. "There's nothing behind it, Cora. Really. It's a door to nowhere."

What a fitting metaphor for our constricted life. She wanted to say the words out loud but there was a touchiness about him since they moved to Idaho, an undercurrent that made her sidestep rather than dive into confrontations.

The first person Damien willingly allowed on their homestead was Frank Barnes, the owner of *The Pig's Tail* on Main Street. D invited Frank to dinner because of his tendency to gossip. What better way to earn the community's trust than have a well-known "prepper" vouch for them?

"Nice," Frank said, devouring Cora's special lamb stew after sniffing it suspiciously beforehand. "Maybe I can add this dish to my menu and name it after you." Cora couldn't tell if he was joking or not. After a few beers the men exchanged conspiracy theories about how the Parkland High School shooting was a hoax perpetrated by actors and the World Trade Center was hit by a missile launched by the government, its collapse a controlled demolition. Cora kept her mouth shut. It was all part of the charade and she hated every moment of it.

Later, Damien and Frank walked the property and Frank saw what he was meant to see—a well-hidden entrance to a fortified shelter in the hillside.

After Damien and Cora had put the kids to bed and were settled on the couch splitting a bottle of beer, he told her how the restaurateur's eyes lit up with approval "at the sight of our fake bunker."

"Didn't Frank want a look inside?"

"You bet. His exact words were, 'mind if I take a gander?' I had trouble keeping a straight face. I can't believe some people still talk that way."

"Maybe he was pulling your leg."

"Nope. He was on the level. I told him I keep the door booby-trapped and it was too much trouble to disarm. He winked at me, like I'm one of the boys. So it's all taken care of. I'm in the club."

She worked up the courage to ask, "Why is being in the club so important?"

Damien slipped an arm around her waist. "The people who live around here, either you're for them or against them. If someone decided I was a government spy they might shoot first and ask questions later."

Damien's ploy worked. Within a week word was out and fewer questioning looks were leveled at Cora when she made her weekly trip to the Food Mart. It looked like the fake bunker had done its job and their family would be left alone.

But like Cora had overheard her English teacher at South Seattle College telling a wannabe gangster student: "We often become what we pretend to be."

A week later, Damien got a call to troubleshoot a rancher's transformer. He gave Cora detailed instructions on what to do if the intruder returned.

Almost as soon as Damien drove off, the trespasser appeared in the same place in the yard, as if she'd watched the house and waited for him to leave. Yes, it was a woman, wearing a green camouflage shirt that matched her baseball hat and holding up a sign with a message in large black letters. **Come out and talk**.

Pulled in two directions, Cora decided she would make her choice with a mental flip of the coin. *If it's heads, I call Damien and if it's tails, I check out this woman on my own.*

Henry had gone to his room after lunch but not Hannah.

"What's that sign mean, Mom? And why aren't you closing the shutters?" Recently, at Damien's insistence, Hannah had started calling her "Mom." Henry still seemed reluctant.

"It's okay sweetheart." Cora tousled the six-year-old's curly black hair and told her that the woman was someone she'd met in town who wanted to talk with her privately. It was then that she realized the coin had already come up tails.

Hannah sulked. "Why can't she come into the house? I promise I'll stay out of the way."

"Maybe she had a fight with her husband and is afraid your father will take his side. You know how men like to stick together. You can watch some TV while I'm gone."

Cora hated lying to the child but lately the contrast between her dream of making a go of it in the country and the reality of their strangely secretive life was making her do some uncharacteristic things.

It was chilly outside and she poured two cups of coffee to bring with her on what already felt like a traitorous excursion. The woman smiled thinly and accepted the steaming cup. Wisps of auburn hair stuck out from under her dark blue baseball cap.

"You must be Cora Jenkins. Pleased to meet you. I'm Agent Scoletti." She showed her FBI badge and ID and waited for Cora to respond.

"Don't you have better things to do than harass people whose only crime is to move to the countryside? We're not who you think we are." All the while she was thinking, *Damien's taken his game of pretend too far and now the government believes he's some kind of armed fanatic.*

"Is that what you expect me to believe? That you're here with your husband to get back to the land?" Agent Scoletti retrieved a folded document from her shoulder bag. As she held it out, the paper flapped in the wind like a trapped bird. "Let me hold your coffee while you read this."

It was a court document, *People of the State of Washington v. Damien Jenkins.*

It took some time for the story behind the printed words to sink in and when it did, Cora sat down hard on the ground, wishing she could sink into the soil and disappear. Damien's dead ex-girlfriend, Samantha Willis, was very much alive and had accused him of kidnapping their children, Hannah and Henry Willis.

Damien had told Cora that he and Samantha were never married and that she had died from an overdose of heroin. Lying to her was bad enough. Letting Hannah and Henry believe their mom was dead seemed cruel beyond belief.

Agent Scoletti minced no words. "If you cooperate it's unlikely you'll face any charges yourself. Here's what I'd like you to do."

Back inside the house, Cora tossed the two coffee cups in the sink and reached for the whisky bottle they kept on the top shelf of the walk-in pantry. To give herself some privacy, she closed the door and sipped on the fortifying drink while she thought over what she'd say to Damien when he got home.

She stayed in the pantry for almost an hour, tidying up to keep from going insane. No matter what solution she considered, she couldn't see a way ahead that didn't involve harm to the kids emotionally and psychologically. They were supposed to come first but Cora had watched the evening news enough to know that in these kinds of situations they never did.

The first thing she noticed when she stepped back into the kitchen was how quiet the house was. The second thing was Damien's truck. For some reason he'd come home early. Had he taken the children for a walk in the woods like he often did, quizzing them on the names of the trees? He was a good father but her view of him was completely changed now that she knew what he'd done. She couldn't afford to think about that now. She had to find them.

Walking across the fields toward the stretch of national park that adjoined their property, she considered what a good hiding place Damien had chosen. There were no neighbors for miles. She'd have to handle this herself before the FBI returned in force. Agent Scoletti had made it clear that the farm was under surveillance. She'd given Cora a day to convince Damien to turn himself in before they came for him. Given the number of guns in their house, that made sense. No one wanted another Ruby Ridge.

She was walking by the hillock covered with poison oak when she noticed how the grass in front was trampled. She pivoted and walked toward the thicket of toxic red and green, three-leaf formations, which also had been disturbed. Her heart raced even before the thought arrived—had he locked himself and the children inside layers of concrete? Could the fake bunker actually be real? Was this the "project" Damien had said he needed to finish before she and the kids could move in?

Cora raised her fist to knock and like magic the metal door swung open. Damien reached out and grabbed her arm, roughly pulling her inside. "So glad you decided to join us," he said, his voice thick with sarcasm as he spun the circular, submarine-style lock, sealing his family inside.

The corrugated metal walls made the room feel like a storage container, and Cora assumed that's what it had been before Damien remodeled it.

Henry and Hannah were sitting at the far end of a built-in bench and they briefly looked up from their Gameboys. He'd thought of everything. No wireless or cellphone access here and the kids would need distracting.

Damien tightened his grip on Cora's arm. "I'm surprised you didn't bring her with you?"

"Who do you mean?"

"Don't play coy with me. That bitch from the FBI who you made a deal with. Do you want to hear the recording?"

So he'd been spying on her and the kids all along. It made sense that the sensors he bragged about would have been wired for audio too.

"Dad, why are you cursing at Cora?" Henry asked.

"It's nothing to concern yourself about. Go back to your game. Like I told you this is just a drill. She doesn't like it but she'll come 'round."

Damien made a show of smiling at Cora, and she sat down next to him on the bench, managing to keep her face neutral. *He doesn't want to scare the kids. That's a good sign.*

"How about a tour?" she asked. "I might as well learn my way around if this is going to be our home for a while. What's the square footage on a place like this anyway?"

"Four hundred. Amazing what you can fit in when you have to."

For a bunker, she had to admit it was well-appointed. Damien showed off the tiny, efficient bathroom and the power supply and she pretended to listen to his long-winded technical explanation of how he'd started out with a storage unit and then expanded by digging into the hillside. "I installed the air vents and put in a power supply myself. The water is filtered and safe for the kids to drink," he added proudly.

He pushed on a section of wall to open an invisible door. "This is the safe room."

She followed him into an area furnished with air mattresses and a large chest of drawers. A dormitory for four.

She shut the door and said softly but firmly, "Your ex-whatever-she-is, Damien. She's not dead."

"Samantha's a drug addict and a thief. We were living in LA. A few weeks after she was sent to rehab by the court, I told the kids that she overdosed and died. By the time she was released, we were long gone. We moved to Seattle to start over. And then I met you. Next to the children, you're the best thing that ever happened to me. I'm sorry I lied. I didn't want to lose you."

His voice was so full and resonant. His face had softened too. It was like speaking the truth after all this time was changing him before her eyes. *This might be the first honest conversation we've ever had. Except that he might still be lying. How would I know?*

She thought of the enthusiastic member of Seattle Tilth she'd fallen in love with while touring the irrigation system on a boutique apple farm. Was her Damien still living somewhere inside this strange man?

"I know what you're thinking, Cora. I should have given Samantha a chance. But the courts always side with the mom, no matter what. And you don't know her. She's an angel from hell who gave birth to the sweetest children on God's earth."

Should she believe him or not? And did it matter now that it was too late to change anything?

"Cora, please say something."

She told him she needed to use the bathroom. Like everything else in the bunker, it was highly functional and minimalistic, except for the two small toothbrushes with brightly colored plastic flowers decorating their handles. Suddenly she knew what to do.

True to her word, Agent Scoletti honored the twenty-four hours of grace time. At 2:00 p.m. the following day she showed up at the house, backed up by four county deputies. Damien was waiting for her on the porch. Cora and the children were gone.

Before he surrendered himself, Damien showed the agents a video Cora had recorded on his phone. Her face was pale and there was an occasional flutter in her delivery, but the words came out strong. "My husband Damien is a good man who did something wrong for the sake of his children. I'm the one who is responsible for them now and I won't let them be taken into the foster care system or returned to their irresponsible mother. I will keep them safe until you release their father, you can be sure of that."

Scoletti watched the recording twice and then handcuffed Damien and put him in one of the squad cars.

"Should we put out an Amber Alert?" one of the deputies asked while they were searching the house. Scoletti surveyed the spotless kitchen and the fridge loaded with healthy vegetables and fruit juice. She looked out the window at Damien's truck, still parked in the driveway. "We don't have a license plate number to circulate. Let's give this a little more time."

Inside the bunker, Cora comforted the children and told them they'd see their father before long. She thought about Frank, who as far as she knew was the only one in town who knew about the metal door set into the hillside. If he was as much of a gossip as Damien claimed, things could get complicated. But for now, they were safe and she'd take it one day at a time.

Contributor

Joyce Yarrow is a New York City transplant now living in Seattle. Joyce began her writing life scribbling poems on the subway and observing human behavior from every walk of life. The author of five novels, she is a Pushcart Prize nominee with short stories and essays that have appeared in *Inkwell Journal, Whistling Shade, Descant, Arabesques, Weber: The Contemporary West,* and the *Los Angeles Review of Books.*

Contributor's Note:
"Idaho Dreams"

In "Idaho Dreams" I explore a longtime preoccupation: how easy it is to be blindsided by love and catapulted into unknown, dangerous territory. If you've ever discovered a friend or a lover's true nature the hard way, then you know what I mean. This kind of rude awakening is often accompanied by a loss of innocence that gradually gives way to a feeling of fatalism. After that there's the matter of disconnecting from the person who has deceived us. Unless, and here's the rub, our beloved turns out to have had a good reason to mislead us. What do we do then? This is the dilemma faced by Cora toward the end of the story.

Writing "Idaho Dreams" also allowed me to venture into the mindset of a would-be "survivalist bunker-builder," by creating a character who tries to take advantage of that stereotype to disguise his own identity. Damien successfully takes on the stripes of a leopard and make the big cats think he's one of them. However, streaks of paint easily wash off in the rain and he needs a more permanent disguise to pull off his fake identity. One question stayed with me until I finished writing—would Damien end up becoming what he at first only pretended to be?

It was inevitable that these two characters have an adversarial relationship but I am not a believer in destiny. The choices Cora and Damien make at the end of the story are a testimony to free will.

Book Publications

Novels

Ask the Dead (Martin Brown Publishing, 2005). Poet-detective Jo Epstein tackles a tangle of money-laundering, kidnapping, and murder while haunted by shadows from her past and guilt over debts unpaid.

Russian Reckoning (published in hardcover as *The Last Matryoshka* by Five Star Mysteries, 2005) Book two in the Jo Epstein series. Roped into helping her émigré stepfather, Nikolai, escape the clutches of a ruthless blackmailer, Jo Epstein must enter a world where criminals enforce a 19th century code of honor, threats arrive inside traditional Matryoshka (nesting) dolls, and fashion models adorn themselves with lewd prison tattoos.

Rivers Run Black (Vitasta Publishing, New Delhi, 2015), co-authored with Arindam Roy. A story of the Indian Diaspora and the search for the American dream, this novel is driven by action and suspense, as well as mythological and psychological themes that intersect and merge at the end.

Zahara and the Lost Books of Light (Adelaide Books, New York, 2020). Seattle journalist Alienor Crespo travels to Spain to claim the promise of citizenship offered to the descendants of Jews expelled from Spain in 1492. As she relives history through her *vijitas* (visits) with her ancestors, Alienor also confronts modern-day extremism and commits herself to protecting an endangered "Library of Light"—a hidden treasure trove of medieval Hebrew and Arabic books saved from the fires of the Inquisition.

Sandstorm (D.X. Varos, Denver, 2021). A story of survival, coming-of-age, and redemption, *Sandstorm* presents an alternative to the traditional family, as Sandie Donovan rebuilds her life with a group of eccentric and loyal friends.

A SPOONFUL OF SOUP

Rita Baker

THE WIND WAS HOWLING. THE morning was dark and menacing with snow ready to fall from a clouded sky onto the streets below. Everyone was bundled up, thick scarves, thick gloves, eyes peeping out from beneath woolen hats.

It was even too cold and windy to stop and place a buck in the beggar's hands that were held out in hope, as he sat, still as a statue, on the frozen sidewalk, wearing an overlarge coat he found in a rubbish bin, ragged woolly gloves with fingers missing; the only covering on his straggly grey hair and beard was the snow now falling fast from the skies above.

Otto swallowed the cough that began rising in his dry and thirsty throat. The door to the restaurant he was sitting close to would soon open, and a hot cup of coffee would be handed to him with a roll or cake left over from the day before. He began to shiver from the extreme cold while waiting, waiting impatiently for the door to open.

"Otto, Otto, come in quick," cried the sous chef from behind the door he held open just a crack.

"You want me to come inside?" questioned Otto, who had never been asked inside before.

"Of course inside, it's much too cold out there today. I have some good warming soup; come in before we get ready for customers."

Struggling to his feet, Otto slowly entered the warm inside. He glanced around. Small tables well-placed, a thick carpet running the length of the floor between tables. Attractive lights hung from a low ceiling giving the room a warm welcoming glow. "Where?" asked Otto, glancing around.

"In the kitchen," pointed the chef, "there is a table behind the door. I'll bring you some warming soup. But you must leave before we open."

Otto breathed in the aromatic air. It had been long since he enjoyed the wonderful aroma of a good restaurant, and he felt choked with the well-remembered sights and smells. The chef sat him down and placed a bowl of hot soup in front of him. His hands shook when he took the spoon and dipped it into the steaming broth, then, taking his first mouthful, he clicked his tongue to taste the brew after swallowing, then with a glance up at the chef said, "Something missing. Um—try a little palm rind, and just a little extra kosher salt."

Raising his eyebrows, the chef asked, "Palm rind? Are you sure? And why kosher salt. What would you know about kosher salt?"

"No questions. Just try, OK?"

"OK," he said, in doubt.

It worked. "What a difference," he cried. "How, how is it that you should know about such things?"

"I have not always been this poor, tired old man. I used to love food, all food, as long as it was well cooked and with the finest ingredients."

"Finest ingredients! My oh my! Now you will have to taste all my soups!"

"It's simple when you know all the little tricks, like lemon juice for flavour, yogurt for a rich taste without using cream, and beer in beef or mushroom. And to roast the meat bones to increase the flavour. There are so many little tricks."

"This is amazing. I need to speak to the boss about it. You know, I just might have an idea."

The next day, Otto was called into the restaurant by the head chef and owner. "How come you know of these little tricks?" he asked.

Otto wasn't certain if he should explain how he came by his vast knowledge of soups, but an explanation was needed, and as difficult as the situation was for him, after giving it much thought, he said, "Um—I used to love food, good food, especially soups, and when you love food, it is a need you have to explore, so I explored."

The head chef stroked his chin. You know what," he said, "I have a deal for you. You can sleep in the shed behind the restaurant, and for your knowledge and advice, you will have all your meals included. What do you say?"

Otto gasped. What could he say? But, he wondered, was being tied down what he wanted? But then again, wasn't he already tied down to a life of poverty and misery?

"OK," he cried. "Yes, yes I accept."

And so it was that Otto became a trusted member of the restaurant staff, giving advice as the taster-in-chief of the soup.

Word about the soup soon got around on the street, bringing in a new lot of customers for the soup alone, and all at once the restaurant went from an obscure little café to a restaurant of quality.

One month, two months, a year went by, and the restaurant went from success to success as it continued to bring in new customers.

It was on one such day, that a delighted customer asked to speak to the chef in charge of the soup, and Otto was brought to his table. The man gasped when he saw him. And Otto, recognizing the man, took a step back in fright.

"Otto, Otto," the customer cried, "is it really you?"

Otto kept shaking his head, crying in fear, "No, no, no. I don't know who you are."

The man was quick to understand and, rising, he shook Otto's hand, then addressed the owner of the restaurant. "Many years ago," he began, "I used to eat at a restaurant where the soup was to die for. The soup I just had, was every bit as good and reminded me of those days. You see, the owner was an absolutely wonderful, top chef, at that time. Otto, here, just reminded me of him, but of course, he is not the man I used to know and respect."

"What happened to the restaurant?" asked the owner.

"Otto, this other Otto, was a heavy gambler, and when he couldn't pay off his debts, the strong-arm-boys were brought in and smashed the restaurant, including the owner's arms. It was the end of one of the finest restaurants in this city. I never thought I would see the day when I would enjoy such soup again, until today. You are a great soup master, sir," he said, addressing Otto, "Thank you, thank you. And may God bless you for returning to me, those wonderful memories, of an unforgettable soup."

A lump formed in Otto's throat, and tears wet his eyes.

Contributor

Rita Baker has lived in Canada since leaving England with her husband to follow their two sons. Reading has been her passion from an early age, Somerset Maugham, H. G. Wells, and, of course, Shakespeare that was drummed into her at school, whose works she also happened to love. Baker writes, "While being a wife and mother is most fulfilling, writing has been my vocation since the age of six when I used to sit before the fire and dream of princes and princesses as depicted in the fairy-tale books that were my passion, and as I grew, so my stories grew with me until, at last, I was able to fulfill my heart's desire to write. Happily, my life has been full of all the things necessary for a writer to draw from, love, joy, heartrending moments of immeasurable pain and heartache, loss, and happily, fulfillment. Everything that living is about, the living that is so necessary to fulfill a writer's heart and mind. I have often heard people casually say, "I think I would like to write a book." While I say nothing, "I think I would like to write a book" comes nowhere close to why a writer writes. It is nothing less than the air you breathe. The warm sun on your face. The moon that traps your heart in its beams. It is the sound of a trumpet in your ears. The song in your heart. The love in your eyes.

It is who you have always wanted to be. It is who someone, on high, decided who you were to be."

Contributor's Note:
"A Spoonful of Soup"

The world may be a happy place for some. Some, but unfortunately, not all. Is it pure luck that you land on your feet, or is it the hard work you put into your dreams, dreams that can be destroyed in a flash by carelessness, complacency or a weakness like gambling that inflicts us from time to time, and we end up ruined, or worse, in the gutter? No self-esteem, no self-respect, no hope of untangling the sticky web that draws us in like a spider out to catch an unsuspecting fly. Horses, Blackjack, the cursed wheel of fortune in a house of sin. Loose women, the devil's temptations, and the weak are lost. Such was the lot of Otto in "A Spoonful of Soup." Feel sorry for the weak, for there, but for the grace of God, go you. Never look down on the weak, for, if you have never been tempted, then you know not what you may be capable of.

Book Publications

Novels

Of Breeding and Birth has elements of love, hate, mystery and romance, and explores the themes of inequality and prejudice as well as the bondage that comes from close family ties, especially between lawyer, Archie Bingham, the main character, and his harsh and unyielding father, a British barrister with a hidden second family.

Born of Love takes the reader on a heartrending journey from Poland, in the early 20th century, to America where Tova, the main character, is illegally spirited into the country by two young men of different backgrounds and the tragic consequences of their action. Yet, despite an horrendous beginning, and against all odds, Tova wins through and becomes a woman to be reckoned with.

My Dear Cousin Sadie, taken from a true story before, during, and after WWII, speaks of the courage of Sadie and what it takes to come to terms with what life dishes out to some who, through no fault of their own, are forced to travel a road full of twists and turns and complexities and yet are still able to find fulfillment and contentment among the debris scattered about them.

Memoir

Victim of Circumstances is an irrational tale of devastation and hope that can come out of the ashes of war; it gives an insight into the life of a European Jewess during WWII and the tragedies she endured created by a man named Hitler.

Poetry

On Love is a volume of poetry centered on feelings, hopes, and passions.

SPEED DIAL

Amy E. Wallen

———❖———

I LET THE PHONE RING. After the tenth or twelfth ring, I tell myself that he's always taken a long time to get to the phone. If I hang up, I take the chance that he may be just about to answer. A 92-year-old can take a long time to get across the room.

Sometimes I let the phone ring while I go about my business, AirPods in my ears with the ringing as a background noise. It's almost like I'm talking to him. Him telling me a story, me partially listening.

The phone company is sending the refund, they said it would arrive in thirty to sixty days. Is that how long I have? One day I will call, and it won't be him that answers. Some stranger will say, "Hello," and I'll say, "Sorry, wrong number."

When there's no answer today, I tell myself that maybe he's just at bingo, and I will call again later.

And I do. I call at least once a week. Maybe I should call every day? I always thought that I should call more often, and never did. I try now. I try to make up for not calling as often as I should have. For not calling just to say hi here and there.

I was never sure if he remembered if I had called. Other times he would accuse me of calling just because I wanted to tell him to behave, to treat the caregivers better, to tell him how much money he had left. He never said, "You don't call just because you care." He never said that.

I let the phone continue to ring and no one answers. I know he's not at bingo. He's not at art class that he went to every Friday. He's not in the dining room. He's not taking a walk. Not on an outing in the little bus. He's not taking too long to get across the room.

He will never answer again. But I will keep calling. Checking to see if one day he will answer. Just in case. Maybe when he answers it will be a different time. I'll be calling to tell him my flight schedule. Maybe I'm calling to find out when he and mom will be arriving. Maybe he will say, "Hey!

I knew it was you." Maybe I will get irritated again that he rambles on. Maybe we will play the game we have played since I left home for college where he and I refuse to be the first one to hang up. We will say goodbye over and over and over and over. "You hang up first." "No, you hang up." "No, you." "No, you."

No, you.

Guest Contributor

Amy Wallen is the author of the best-selling novel, *MoonPies & Movie Stars* (Penguin 2007), and the memoir, *When We Were Ghouls: A Memoir of Ghost Stories* (University of Nebraska 2018). Her sardonic look at writing and its demands, and her mad love of pie come together in her third book, *How to Write a Novel in 20 Pies: Sweet & Savory Secrets from the Writing Life* (Andrews McMeel October 2022). As writer-in-residence at Ocean Discovery Institute, Amy teaches personal storytelling to young people traditionally excluded from science due to race, income status, and educational opportunity. She also provides book editing services for persevering writers.

Contributor's Note: "Speed Dial"

After my father died this year, his phone number popped up in my recently called numbers so I dialed the number out of curiosity to see what would happen. After the first time, I started calling it regularly to listen to it ring. After many years of taking care of him long distance and having to wait for him to get to the phone, I find comfort in knowing I can still call and wait, albeit forever, for him to pick up. Maybe it's hope he'll answer, maybe it's despair that I can never talk to him again, or maybe it's just a small moment of reaching out to something familiar—a distant flicker of someone I wish was still there.

Acknowledgments

THE PUBLISHER THANKS THE TELLTALE AUTHORS' group for providing the initial spark of inspiration that became *Distant Flickers: Stories of Identity & Loss*. This group provided invaluable help in curating and editing a set of varied stories—each compelling in its own right—into a unified and engaging whole. Without Telltale Authors' ongoing help and support, *Distant Flickers* would not have been possible.

Telltale Authors is a group of writers who came together to give their readers something extra—a look behind the scenes at the inspiration, life experiences, research, and serendipity that went into the creation of the books their readers enjoy.

THE EDITORS OFFER THEIR SINCERE THANKS and appreciation to poet and novelist John Casey for his poem "Empty Skies" to introduce the anthology's theme of identity and loss. The following lines from "Empty Skies" inspired the title of the anthology:

> Where
> a distant flicker somehow marks
> the infinite reach of solitude.

John Casey is a Pushcart Prize-nominated poet and novelist from New Hampshire. A Veteran combat and test pilot, Casey also served as a Diplomat and International Affairs Strategist at U.S. embassies in Germany and Ethiopia, the Pentagon, and elsewhere. He is inspired by the incredible spectrum of people, places and cultures he has experienced in life.

Book Publications

Poetry

Raw Thoughts: A Mindful Fusion of Poetic and Photographic Art—a nominee for the National Book Award and Griffin Poetry Prize. Each successive poem-photo pairing within (each 'raw thought') builds on an underlying philosophy that compels us to assess and adjust what and how we think with the aim of improving our lives and by extension, the lives of those around us.

Meridian: A Raw Thoughts Book. Meridian addresses analysis and improvement of thought in a manner that is less emotive and more refined than in *Raw Thoughts*, an approach that is cognitive to an extent that most will not instinctively endeavor to pursue. This lends itself naturally to a next-level pursuit of clarity and personal growth.

Novels

Devolution: Book One of The Devolution Trilogy— Michael Dolan is a stoic perfectionist and former special operations pilot working a staff job at the Pentagon. After accepting an improbable CIA offer to help prevent impending terrorist attacks in Europe, Dolan finds that of the demons he must prevail against, the most terrible are those from within.

Evolution: Book Two of The Devolution Trilogy— Two years have passed since the dramatic conclusion of Operation EXCISE. Dolan has moved home to Boston to mend when once again, the Agency comes knocking. Terrorists have launched a bioweapon in the Middle East, thousands are dying of a horrifying virus with no cure, and Dolan is the key to preventing more attacks. Only this time, everything will be done on his terms.

Revelation: Book Three of the Devolution Trilogy—Michael Dolan is now leading the CIA black operations team formerly known as SCALPEL, his fortunes buoyed by unparalleled success in thwarting numerous terrorist attacks. After uncovering a sinister network of organizations planning a cyberattack with global financial and geopolitical implications, he must risk putting the world at war if he is to save it.

Novella

The Barn: A Novella Mystery (co-authored by Doug Campbell and John Casey)—With his mother's health in decline, Keith Conway returns home to New Hampshire. A cryptic message from her makes him question whether his grandfather's accidental death may have in fact been a murder. The more he finds, the more he wonders if it might be best for all to just leave the truth buried.